"We've made it this far. Don't give up."

Heather glanced down. The men had slowed their pace.

"The real danger will be at the bottom of the mountain on the other side. They can get around to there with their ATVs faster than we can get down. They'll be waiting to ambush us."

She tensed. "When will this stop?"

"We are witnesses, Heather. Willis is not going to let us out of the high country alive."

Her stomach tightened into a knot.

Zane grabbed her at the elbows and pulled her toward him. The look in his eyes intensified. "I know you want to give up. But hold on. Can you do that for me?"

She nodded, but felt as though her knees would buckle.

He drew her into his arms. "You're smart and strong. You got me out of that bunker. We can do this."

His arms enveloped her. She melted into the warmth of his embrace, breathing in the scent of his skin. "I just don't see how."

Ever since she found the Nancy Drew books with the pink covers in her country school library, **Sharon Dunn** has loved mystery and suspense. Most of her books take place in Montana, where she lives with three nearly grown children and a spastic border collie. She lost her beloved husband of twenty-seven years to cancer in 2014. When she isn't writing, she loves to hike surrounded by God's beauty.

Books by Sharon Dunn

Love Inspired Suspense

BIG SKY
SHOWDOWN

SHARON DUNN

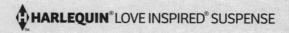
HARLEQUIN® LOVE INSPIRED® SUSPENSE

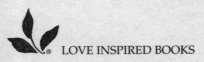

LOVE INSPIRED BOOKS

Recycling programs
for this product may
not exist in your area.

ISBN-13: 978-0-373-45680-2

Big Sky Showdown

How great is the love the Father has lavished on us
that we should be called children of God.
—1 John 3:1

For Susan, Kathy and Jenny, my cheerleaders and fellow suffering artists. For the inspiration, the feedback and the accountability.

ONE

Fear skittered across Heather Jacobs's nerves as half a dozen birds fluttered into the morning sky. Something had spooked them. She gripped the firewood she'd gathered a little tighter. She was alone here. Her guide, Zane Scofield, had taken his rifle, binoculars and hostility and left muttering something about scouting for elk for the next bunch of hunters he would guide into the high country of Montana.

This trip was to take her up to fulfill the last request of the father she barely knew. Five days ago, a certified letter had come to her home in California. Her father's dying wish was that she spread his ashes in his favorite spot in the Montana mountains and that Zane, the outfitter who had worked for Stephan Jacobs, be the one to guide her to the spot on Angel Peak. Heather hadn't seen her father since she was five years old. Her memories of him were faint. Her mother, who had died over a year ago, had never had anything nice to say about her ex-husband.

A brushing sound behind her caused Heather to whirl around. The logs she held rolled from her arms. Her heartbeat revved up a notch. The hairs on the back of her neck stood at attention. She sensed another being nearby.

What kinds of wild animals lurked in the forest?

Now she really wished Zane was closer. He knew how to deal with wildlife. Even if they'd been on each other's nerves since they left Fort Madison two days ago, she at least felt physically safe when he was around.

She stood as still as a statue, listening to the sound of the creaking trees and the drumming of her pulse in her ears.

Taking in a breath, she leaned over to pick up the firewood she'd dropped. Again, she heard what sounded like something moving toward her. She straightened, her gaze darting everywhere. Adrenaline charged through her, commanding her to run.

The smart thing to do would be to head back to the safety of the fire and camp and maybe even find Zane. A flash of something neon yellow caught her eye. Not a color that occurred in nature. Her heart skipped a beat. Whatever was out there was human. For a moment, she found that reassuring. Better a human than a wild animal. But then apprehension returned. Just who was out here, and why did they seem to be following her?

She saw blond hair for a quick second. A yelp as though someone were in pain filled the forest. The cry sounded childlike. Concerned, she ran toward where she'd seen the movement. Crashing noises up ahead alerted her as another moan of pain filled the forest.

Was a child hurt? Afraid?

She sprinted in the general direction of the noises, running around the trees and ducking out of the way of low-hanging branches. She saw the flash of blond again, a boy. More than ten years old, she would guess—but not by much. Perhaps twelve or thirteen.

She caught only fleeting glimpses of the child in the early-morning light.

She came into a clearing as silence descended once again. Her heartbeat drummed in her ears. She pivoted one way and then the other, searching.

"Please come out. I won't hurt you." The thought of a child in distress made her chest tight. What if he was lost and separated from his family?

She caught movement and heard footsteps to the side of her. She turned, expecting to see the blond boy. Instead, an older, darker-haired teenager emerged from the trees with a knife raised above his head and teeth bared. Terror swept over her like a wave.

She turned and bolted away. She may not be used to this environment, but her work as a personal trainer meant she was in top athletic condition. She could outrun the violence that pursued her.

The blond boy emerged from the other side of the forest, also wielding a knife. He wasn't injured. She'd been tricked into going deeper into the forest by these two. But why? What did they want from her?

They gave her little choice as to what direction she could run. She turned sharply and sprinted, willing her legs to move faster. Her heart pounded against her rib cage as she increased her speed.

She glanced over her shoulder. The boys gained on her by only a few yards. She ran faster. She could run all day if she had to.

The trees thinned.

Her foot slipped as the ground beneath her gave way. She found herself twirling through space and colliding with the hard earth as she landed on her back. She stared up at the blue sky and swaying tree boughs. With the wind knocked out of her, it took her a moment to comprehend that she'd fallen in a deep hole that had been camouflaged with brush and evergreen branches.

Her eyes traced over the twenty feet of dirt wall on either side of her that held her prisoner. She tilted her head to where the sunlight sneaked through the trees.

A grinning face appeared overhead, blond hair wild and uncombed. The child looked almost feral. They'd forced her in this direction so she'd fall in the hole.

Fear snaked around her torso and caused her to shiver. Now that she was their prisoner, what did they intend to do to her?

The blond boy shook his head, still smiling, pleased with himself. He formed a gun with his fingers, aimed it at her and mimed pulling the trigger. She winced against such a dark action from someone so young.

The older, darker-haired boy popped his head over the edge of the hole. He high-fived the younger kid.

"Dude, we're so going to get extra rations for this," said the older boy.

The blond boy continued to grin as he gazed down at her. "Maybe even a promotion."

"You stay here and guard her," said the older boy. "I'll head up to the patrol station so they can radio it in to base camp."

Patrol? Base camp? That sounded like they were part of an organized group. That meant more were coming, and they probably weren't boys. A chill enveloped Heather that had nothing to do with the crisp fall morning. She wasn't rich or famous—they couldn't hope to hold her for ransom. But the other possibilities for why they would want to kidnap her made blood freeze in her veins.

The older boy disappeared as suddenly as he'd appeared. The blond boy wiped his knife on his pants and stepped away as well. She could hear him above her pacing back and forth, breaking twigs beneath his feet.

Heart racing, she stared up the slick, steep walls. If she could get out, she should be able to overtake or outrun the blond boy. She needed to hurry before the others got here. She positioned her foot in the side of the dirt wall and tried to climb. She slipped. There was nothing to hold on to but moist earth.

The boy popped his head over the edge of the hole again. "You can't get out, lady. Don't even try."

"Why are you doing this?"

He sneered at her in a sinister way. Her heart seized up.

She was trapped. Her only hope was that Zane would get back to camp soon, see that she wasn't there and come looking for her. That was a thin hope at best.

Zane Scofield stared through his high-powered binoculars, scanning the hills and mountains all around him. He did need to scout for elk for future trips, but he also had to get away from Heather before he lost it. Just the thought of her made him grit his teeth.

Most of what Heather knew about her father had come through the bitter lens of her mother who had left a drunk in Montana twenty years ago. That was not the Stephan Jacobs whom Zane had come to know seven years ago. The Stephan whom Zane had worked for and been a friend to had been sober and loved God with all his heart.

When Heather had shown up at Big Sky Outfitters, dressed simply in jeans and a sweater, he had wondered what such a beautiful woman was doing on his doorstep. Then of course, she'd ruined that good first impression by talking down the man who had saved Zane's life in more ways than one.

There was no reply Zane could make to her snide comments, wondering why Stephan had left Big Sky Outfitters to her when he'd supposedly "never cared" about her anyway. Zane was sure that wasn't the truth—but he couldn't contradict her when he didn't know the whole story. Men like Stephan were not in the habit of sharing their pain. Zane suspected that a twenty-year estrangement from a daughter was one of those wounds that never healed. Maybe that's why the older man had never mentioned her.

And to make things worse, she'd told him that she intended to sell the business to a competitor, who Zane knew cared more about making money than sharing the beauty of God's creation with people. Stephan's legacy would be marred by a man like Dennis Havre.

Zane wanted to honor Stephan's dying wishes to bring his daughter to the chosen spot to scatter the ashes because the man had meant so much to him, but being with Heather for three more days might be his undoing.

He'd also come up to this vantage point for another reason. For the last day or so, he'd had the strange sense that they were being watched. Bow-hunting season didn't open up for a couple more weeks, so only extreme backpackers and men on scouting expeditions were likely to be up in the high country this time of year. So who had been stalking them and why?

He saw movement through his binoculars and focused in. Several ATVs were headed down the mountain toward the campsite where he'd left Heather alone. The speed at which they moved, like they knew where the camp was, set alarm bells off for Zane. He zeroed in on one of the ATVs and saw the handmade flag flying on the back end of it. He knew that flag. His mind was sucked back in time seven years ago to when he had lived in these mountains as a scared seventeen-year-old. If this was who he thought it was, Heather was in danger.

He jumped up from his concealed position and bolted down the steep incline. A thunderstorm of emotion brewed inside him. If he hadn't met Stephan when he did, his life could have gone in a much different direction, and those ATVs reminded him of everything he'd left behind.

Seven years ago, Zane and his brother, Jordan, had escaped foster care and been taken in by a man named Willis Drake. Willis saw a conspiracy around every corner and thought being armed to the teeth and living in the forest would keep him and his followers safe.

At first, Willis had seemed like the father Zane had longed for, teaching him how to shoot and how to live in the wild. If he hadn't taken the job with Stephan, he would have continued to idolize Willis and buy into his crazy theories.

Once authorities tried to catch Willis doing something illegal, Willis and his followers left the area. That had been nearly seven years ago. Now it looked like he might be back. That was frightening enough on its own. But for Willis and his gang to be headed toward where Heather was… That was downright terrifying. He had to keep her safe from that lawless group.

He raced down from his high spot and rushed through the trees to the open area of camp. The fire was burned down to nothing more than hot coals. Both pack mules were still tethered to trees. Heather was gone. Pushing away the rising panic, he sprinted toward a different part of the forest where he had directed her to find firewood. He spotted several logs together as though they'd been dropped.

He could hear the ATVs drawing closer, but not coming directly into the camp. They were headed a little deeper into the forest. He ran toward the mechanical sound, pushing past the rising fear.

He called for Heather only once. He stopped to listen.

He heard her call back—faint and far away, repeating his name. He ran in the direction of the sound with his rifle still slung over his shoulder. When he came to the clearing, he saw a boy not yet in his teens throwing rocks into a hole and screaming, "Shut up. Be quiet."

Zane held his rifle up toward the boy. He could never shoot a child, but maybe the threat would be enough.

The kid grew wide-eyed and snarled at him. "More men are coming. So there." Then the boy darted into the forest, yelling behind him, "You won't get away."

Zane ran over to the hole. Heather gazed up at him, relief spreading across her face.

Voices now drifted through the trees, men on foot headed this way.

Zane grabbed an evergreen bough and stuck it in the hole for Heather to grip. She climbed agilely and quickly. He grabbed her hand and pulled her the rest of the way out. "We have to get out of here."

There was no time to explain the full situation to her, but he tasted bile every time he thought about what might be going on. His worst nightmare coming true, his past reaching out to grab him by the feet and pull him into a deep dark hole. The past he thought he'd escaped.

He led Heather through the trees back to the camp where the mules were tied up. They mounted and took off, bolting for the trail just as several men burst into the camp on foot. One of them lifted his handgun and aimed it at them but didn't fire. "Stop right there."

Zane spurred his mule into a trot and Heather fell in beside him.

He had no idea why Heather had been targeted by Willis. He only knew one thing. If Willis was back in the high country, no good could come of staying here. He needed to get Heather to safety and fast. He knew what Willis was capable of. Their lives depended on getting out of the high country.

TWO

Heather's thoughts raced a hundred miles an hour as the trail narrowed and grew steeper. Confusion and fear battled within her. What was going on? Who were those men? And where were they going? Zane had told her this morning that they were only half a day away from where she could spread her father's ashes, and now it looked like they were headed back into town, back to Fort Madison.

He dropped back and allowed Heather to go ahead of him on the trail as it became too narrow to ride side by side. Though they slowed down when the terrain became more dangerous, the mules traversed the steep inclines and switchbacks with ease. Above them was rocky mountainside. Below, the trail dropped off at nearly ninety degrees.

She tightened the reins to stop Clarence, her mule, and craned her neck looking past Zane at the trail behind them. The men had not followed them.

Zane drew his eyebrows together. "Keep moving, Heather." Panic tainted his words.

He seemed to know more than he was letting on.

"They didn't follow us," she said, but she turned

back to face the trail ahead of her and nudged Clarence to start moving again. It would be nuts to think of going to Angel Peak knowing that there were crazy men like that up here. Still, she felt a sense of defeat that they'd had to turn back when they were so close to their goal. She'd been on an emotional roller coaster since she'd learned of her father's dying wishes. On some level, she'd come to Montana looking for answers. If Stephan—she couldn't bring herself to call him Dad—had loved her enough to leave her everything, why hadn't he gotten in touch with her when he was alive? She wanted to be a good daughter even if he hadn't been a good father, but she wanted this trip to be over so she could sell Big Sky Outfitters and return to her life in California.

Clarence lumbered along.

"Make him go faster. Just because we don't see them doesn't mean they've given up," Zane said.

After she kicked Clarence with her heels to get him going, she shouted over her shoulder, "You seem to know who these men are." Maybe there had been local news stories she wasn't privy to?

"I'll explain later. Just go. Keep moving." The sense of urgency never left his voice.

Heather glanced up the rocky incline as a rumble turned into a roar. Rocks from above them cascaded down the mountain like a waterfall. An avalanche of rocks was coming straight toward her. She spurred Clarence to go faster. Her chest squeezed tight with terror and all the air left her lungs. Rocks crashed against each other. A tremendous thundering noise surrounded her.

Clarence backed up then bucked. She slid off, falling not just off the mule but off the path altogether, tumbling down the side of the mountain. The crashing was all around her as rocks pelted her legs and arms.

Finally, her body came to a stop. The dust settled. She stared up at blue sky, trying to take in what had just happened. The mules brayed on the trail above her but didn't run. A heavy weight pressed on her leg. The rest of her body felt sore and bruised.

Zane made his way down to her, pulling rocks off her leg where she was trapped. His voice was filled with concern when he asked, "Can you move it?"

Still stunned, she wiggled her foot. "I think I'm just a little beat up."

He reached out a hand for her. "They caused the avalanche to block the trail. I saw more men up there." He pulled her to her feet.

So the rockslide hadn't been an accident.

"There's no time to clear it. I'm sure they'll be coming down after us. We'll get back to Fort Madison another way." So Zane's plan *was* to take her back to town. He climbed up over the rocks then craned his neck back down at her.

Heather moved to follow him but the pain from the bruising slowed her.

"Hurry." He climbed back up to where the mules stood.

Still a little shaken, she followed. No way could the same men who had come for them in camp have gotten ahead of them on the trail. That meant there must be even more of them chasing Zane and her. She could not process what was happening.

Zane turned his mule around on the narrow trail and then helped her get Clarence faced downward, as well. The mules were calm again. She stared back down the trail. Were they headed into a trap? Those other men who had come after them in the camp must still be around.

Her gaze traveled up the steep incline where the rockslide had started, but she saw no movement or any sign of people. She and Zane hurried down the trail and through flatter open country. Every now and then, she glanced over her shoulder, expecting to see men behind her. Nothing. And yet, Zane pushed on.

They rode for several more hours, slowing down as the mules fatigued.

Then, for no reason Heather could tell, Zane sat up straighter in the saddle. His hand brushed over the holster that held his pistol.

The action sent a new wave of terror through her. What was he sensing that she didn't pick up on?

He spurred his mule, but the animal continued to plod along.

"They need to rest," she said.

A strange popping sound shattered the silence. Zane's mule's front legs buckled. Heather's heart filled with horror as the animal collapsed on the ground. The mule had been shot through the head.

"Dismount. You're an easy target," Zane shouted at her. He dragged his legs out from under the dead animal and pulled out his pistol. He needed to keep Heather safe, out of the gun battle that was about to take place.

Heather shook her head. She stayed mounted on a frightened Clarence, who stepped side to side jerking his head anxiously. Heather's gaze was fixed on the dead mule. Shock must be setting in for her. He had to pull her from the paralysis before she became unable to make life-saving decisions or follow his orders.

"Get down then. Get off of there." He turned in a half circle, watching the trees, using his skills to pick apart each section, probing for movement.

She slipped out of her saddle and pressed in close to him. "What's going on?" Her voice trembled.

Zane surveyed the landscape. "The shooter is probably getting into position to line up another shot. That gives us a minute." And a chance at escape. He glanced at Clarence, debating his options. They might be a target if they got back on him. But the mule would give them speed.

Another rifle shot penetrated the forest close to Clarence. The mule whinnied and took off at a gallop, crashing through the trees. At least he hadn't been killed, but the shooter had taken out their best chance to get away fast.

Another shot shattered the air around them. The percussive noise beat against his eardrums and made his heart pound. The bullet stirred up the ground around Heather. She gasped and moved closer to him.

Zane grabbed Heather's hand and pulled her toward the brush for cover. "Run," he ordered her.

Though he saw nothing when he looked over his shoulder, he could detect the human noises behind them, heavy footfalls and the rustle of tree boughs being pushed out of the way. The shooter was on the move, coming after them.

He let go of her hand so they could both run faster. His feet pounded over the pine-needle-laden ground.

They ran for a long time without stopping. Heather

kept up a steady pace. He had to hand it to her. Even after the bruising she'd suffered in the rockslide, the woman could run.

He lagged behind then slowed his pace to catch his breath. "I think we lost him."

She stopped to listen, tilting her head. Then her gaze fell on him. "Who are these men?" Her eyes seemed to look right through him. "You know who they are, don't you?"

A heaviness pressed on his shoulders and chest. How could he begin to explain? He narrowed his eyes at Heather. He barely knew her. What if they were after Heather for some reason? She was the one they'd tried to take captive.

Some distance away, a human voice yelped as though the man had run into something. Zane's muscles tensed as he peered over his shoulder.

He saw Heather's eyes grow wide with fear, and then she started sprinting down the trail, with Zane following on her heels. She jumped over a tree that had fallen across the path. Zane hurried to catch up with her.

He heard a noise to the side of him. Two muscular young men jumped out of the trees. One grabbed Zane's hands before he could react. The other placed a hood over his head and pulled Zane's pistol out of the holster. Zane twisted from side to side trying to get away.

The last noise he heard was Heather's scream.

THREE

Stunned and afraid, Heather watched as the men dragged Zane deeper into the forest. She rushed to get back over the log, determined to free him.

A third man appeared from out of the trees and came charging toward her. She had no choice but to run the other way.

The horror of seeing Zane taken captive plagued her as she sprinted off the trail and into the forest. Running hard, she pushed through the tangle of trees. Despite her speed, her feet hit the ground with precision as she chose her steps over the varied terrain. Her pursuer stayed within yards of her but never gained on her. She looped back around to the trail where it would be easier to put some distance between herself and the man.

She bolted up the trail, running for at least twenty minutes before she looked over her shoulder and saw no one. The man had given up. She slowed to a jog. Now that she was safe, her only thought was to help Zane.

Aware that another pursuer might be lying in wait, she stumbled toward where she'd seen the young men drag Zane. There were at least three men, two that had taken Zane and one who had come after her. Even if one of them had been the shooter, what about the other men and boys they'd seen? Just how many people were after them? With each turn in the trail, she feared she'd be caught in another violent encounter.

But after wandering for what seemed like ages, she was less worried about a confrontation and more worried about never finding anyone at all. All the trees along the trail looked the same. If she could find the log that had fallen across the trail, she might be able to figure out where Zane had been taken. But she did not know these woods. Zane was the navigator.

A heaviness descended on her. Zane could be miles from here by now, or worse…he could be dead. Her stomach knotted at the thought. She wiped it from her mind. Giving in to fear would only make things harder.

She pushed off the tree and jogged out to the path. If she worked her way back to the clearing where Zane's mule was shot, she might be able to retrace her steps to where Zane had been taken.

As she followed the trail, she fought against the images that threatened to make her shut down. Pictures of Zane shot and left for dead played through her mind.

She stumbled into the clearing where the dead mule still lay. Her stomach roiled at the sight, and she thought she might vomit. She whirled away, but not before she noticed that the saddlebags and Zane's rifle had been taken.

Turning in a half circle, she wondered if she was being watched. Her own intense heartbeat drummed in her ears.

At least from here, she thought she could find her way back to the fallen log. The memory of fleeing after the shots were fired was blurred by trauma. All the same, she took off in the general direction she remembered going. She'd gone only a short distance when she heard a crashing noise to the side of her. Scrambling to find cover, she slipped behind a tree. Heather pressed her back against the rough bark as her heart thudded at breakneck pace.

She held her breath. The noise of someone moving toward her intensified. Her muscles tensed. The forest fell silent. She waited. Then she heard a familiar *clomp clomp clomp*.

Heather almost laughed as she raised her head. Clarence stood on the path. He jerked his head at her. The metal on his bridle jangled.

"Hello, old friend." She rose to her feet. The saddlebags were askew, but still intact. She opened one and took out the little wooden box that contained her father's ashes. She placed it in the inside pocket of her coat where it pressed against her stomach so she could feel that it was safe. She had been only a short time away from closing this chapter of her life. So much had changed so quickly. Tears welled up. Why had her father wanted her to come back to Montana anyway? She wiped her eyes.

Come on, Heather, pull it together.

Her eyes were drawn to a bloody gash on Clarence's neck. The mule sidestepped when she placed her hand near the injury. She couldn't discern the cause of the wound. It could be a bullet had grazed him, or maybe he'd scraped it on some brush. She straightened the saddlebags and placed her foot in the stirrup. Heather rode a short way when she saw smoke rising off in the distance. A camp.

She spurred Clarence to go faster.

Once they'd gotten close, she slipped off Clarence's back. It could be another hunters' camp doing some scouting or it could be where Zane was being held. Or the men who had been after them might be there without Zane. It could be a chance for help or she could be stepping into danger. Either way, she had to find out.

She let the reins fall to the ground, opting not to tie Clarence up. At least if she did not come back, the mule would be able to find his way back to civilization. And not coming back was a high probability.

She pressed her boots lightly on the crunchy snow, moving toward the rising smoke. Before she even arrived at the camp, she heard voices. Though she couldn't discern the words, it was clear a heated discussion was taking place. She slowed her pace even more, choosing where she stepped carefully. The scent of wood smoke filled the air. The argument stopped and the voices fell silent.

Flashes of color and movement caught her attention. She sank to the ground to take in the scene. Though the trees obscured some of her view, she caught a glimpse of a young man pacing, the hue of his greasy light blue coat distinctive enough to separate him from the forest colors.

Her throat constricted with fear. She recognized him as one of the men who had taken Zane. And there was another boy there, too, though she couldn't see him—she just heard the sound of his voice, mingled with the static of a radio transmitting.

The young man in the blue coat was clearly distressed, hunched, moving in an erratic pattern and slapping his forehead with his hands. She shifted her position, hoping to spot Zane.

Bluecoat tossed another log on the fire and stood close to it. At first, she thought the man had on red gloves, but then she saw that his hands were red from the cold. His tennis shoes probably didn't do much to keep the autumn chill out either.

Bluecoat turned and spoke to a spot that was just outside of Heather's field of vision. "What did he say?"

The other boy replied. "He doesn't trust us to bring him in. He's sending Mason and Long to come and get him. He's mad we didn't get the girl."

Heather breathed a sigh of relief. They had to be talking about Zane. And from what they'd said, it sounded as if Zane was still alive. And even better, it looked like there were only two young men guarding him for now. The third one, the one who had chased her, must have taken off.

Bluecoat threw up his hands. "Oh, sure, and then they get all the credit. While we have to go back out on patrol."

"You know what Willis says. You gotta earn it." The second kid stepped closer to the fire. He was taller than Bluecoat, though just as ragged looking in a tattered brown parka and worn combat boots. At least he had some gloves. Heather guessed he might be eighteen or nineteen years old. "They'll be down here in seven to ten minutes."

Heather moved in a little closer. Her foot cracked a twig. Both boys stiffened, stepped away from the fire and glanced around nervously.

Though she was in an uncomfortable position, she tucked her arms close to her body and didn't move. Her heart beat so loudly, she was afraid it would give her away. Her front foot strained to maintain balance.

Both boys skirted the camp, searching the area before returning to the fire.

Heather exhaled. She waited until they started talking again before she crept in a circle around their camp trying to find Zane. She hurried from tree to tree to remain hidden.

"How long before they get here?" Bluecoat stepped even closer to the fire.

"A few minutes. I told you that. They're coming on the ATVs to haul him up," said Browncoat.

Both young men had handguns in holsters fastened to their belts. She recognized Zane's pistol on the second man. She edged a little closer, finally spotting Zane far from the fire. The pillowcase was still on his head. His hands were tied behind his back. He wasn't slumped over, which she hoped meant that he was conscious.

She moved farther away from the center of the camp and then circled around to where Zane was. The rumble of the ATVs filled the air. Still some distance away, but she knew she didn't have much time.

She scooted through the evergreens until she was lined up with the tree where Zane was tied. Each time she took a step forward, she waited until the conversation intensified to cover the sound of her movement.

Her eyes fixated on Zane's hands where they were bound behind the narrow trunk of a lodgepole pine. Crouching, she positioned herself so most of her body was hidden behind Zane.

Zane must have sensed something was up because his head jerked. The action was enough to cause the conversation between the two men to trail off. She pressed her belly against the ground, shielding herself behind Zane.

She squeezed her eyes shut as the footsteps came toward them. Her heart pounded out a wild rhythm. The footsteps stopped several feet away. She assumed the guard was scanning the area, though she wasn't bold enough to sit up and check. After a few moments he walked away, and then the conversation resumed.

She brushed her hand over Zane's, hoping he would understand. He gave her a thumbs-up. She pulled her pocketknife from her jeans' pocket and cut him free.

The roar of the ATVs pressed on her ears. More voices carried through the trees after the engines died. Two more men entered the camp. All the men were facing away from Zane. Now was their chance for escape.

Zane reached up and tore off the hood, taking no more than an instant to orient himself before he turned and slipped into the trees with Heather.

He breathed a prayer of thanks that Heather had been so smart and brave in breaking him free.

Adrenaline kicked into high gear as he jumped to his feet and sprinted alongside her. Behind him, shouting and protest rose up. Then a single wild gunshot echoed through the trees.

"Don't kill them!" one of the men ordered. "Willis wants them alive."

Zane caught up with her as they raced toward an open area. The ATVs roared to life. They needed to get to terrain where the machines couldn't follow them. She glanced around.

He pointed toward a rocky incline. She hurried after him just as one of the ATVs burst through the trees.

Another bullet whizzed past his ear. They slipped behind a rock and pressed low to the ground. Killing them might not be an option, but wounding them must still be on the table. Zane and Heather pushed themselves upward, using the larger rocks for cover.

They rushed toward the top of the incline. When he glanced down over his shoulder, he saw that one of the men had a high-powered rifle. It was pointed right at him—but before the sniper could take the shot, they reached the ridgeline and headed down the other side.

They sprinted down the grassy side of the hill until they entered a cluster of trees.

Both of them gasped for breath.

Zane ran his hand through his hair and paced as adrenaline coursed through him. "We need to get out of here. It's just a matter of minutes before they catch up with us."

"Who are those guys and why did they kidnap you?"

Her question felt like a weight on his chest. She'd saved his life. He owed her an explanation, but there was no time for that now. "The trail on up the mountain is blocked by the rockslide, so we'll have to go by way of the river."

He didn't wait for her to respond. Instead, he turned and bolted through the trees. If she wanted to stay alive, she'd follow him. She'd already proven she had good survival skills.

The landscape bounced in front of him as he kept pace with Heather.

The sound of the ATVs grew louder then died out and then intensified again. Heather and Zane entered a wide meadow. An ATV emerged from the opposite side of the meadow. Its rider came to a stop and yanked a rifle from a holder attached to the ATV.

Zane grabbed her and pulled her toward the thick evergreens. The first rifle shot stirred the ground up in front of her feet. She jumped back. Zane tugged on her sleeve. Both of them dived toward the shelter of the heavy brush as the sound of more ATV engines filled the forest. The mechanical roar pressed on him from every side. He wasn't sure which way to go to get away. Were they being surrounded?

Zane hesitated for only a moment before choosing a path. They scrambled downward through the trees. The steep path they were on couldn't be called a trail, which would make it that much harder to be followed. The noise of the ATVs died out again. Though he doubted the pursuers had given up.

They jogged until they were both out of breath and needed to stop.

A sense of urgency pressed in on Zane as he pointed off in the distance. "We need to go to the river and get across that bridge. We don't have much time before they catch up with us."

Looking over to the side, he saw where the ATVs snaked down a distant hill. Far enough away for now—but closing in, faster than he and Heather could possibly move on foot.

"How are you going to get to the river? We can't outrun them." Her voice trembled with panic.

As if on cue, a braying noise alerted both of them as Clarence entered the flat area where they stood.

"Looks like our ride's here." Heather hurried over and patted Clarence's neck. "I found him earlier. I'm starting to really like this old mule."

"They always find their way back," Zane said. "Let's drop some of this weight." He reached for the saddlebags.

He pulled a few essential items out and stuffed them into his pockets before yanking the bags off the mule and tossing them on the ground. "We'd better hurry."

A moment later, the sound of the ATVs engines clanging filled the forest around them growing louder and closer. He mounted Clarence and reached out a hand for her to get on behind him. Zane spurred Clarence into a trot. The animal was surefooted enough on the rough terrain that he was able to keep a steady pace. But would be fast enough for them to get away?

Heather wrapped her arms around Zane's waist and pressed close to him. She buried her face in his shoulder-length hair, melting into the warmth of his back. The solid shape of the box that held her father's ashes pushed against her stomach. Until that moment, she'd almost forgotten it was there. Saying goodbye to the father she never knew and finding some closure seemed like the furthest thing from her mind.

They needed to get off this mountain alive. Judging from how ragged and dirty the men and boys all looked, they must live up in the mountains for extended periods. That meant they knew how to survive in the harshness of the high country.

The rushing roar of the river greeted her ears even before she saw the cold gray water and the bridge.

Zane turned his head slightly. "Dismount. We'll lead Clarence across. You go in front of me."

She slid off the mule. The bridge was primitive; the railings were made of narrow but strong cording. The bottom was fashioned from logs bound together with the same cording, stretching across the wide rushing water, connected at either end to sturdy trees. It swayed when she stepped on it. She steadied herself by grabbing the rope railing. Zane fell in behind her, leading Clarence, who hesitated only a moment before he stepped on the unsteady structure.

The ATV noises stopped nearby. The shouts and cries of men out for violence filled the forest. Before long, two of the men emerged through the trees. One of them drew a handgun and shot. The shot went wild. All the same, the gunfire made her stutter in her step.

"Keep going," Zane urged, and he peered over his shoulder.

They were halfway across the bridge.

She couldn't see around him or the mule on the narrow bridge but the look on his face when he turned back around indicated that something had alarmed him.

"What is it?"

"Hurry! The men started to cross and backed up."

Then she heard it—an awful creaking. The bridge swayed. It was unstable and about to break.

They couldn't go back.

She lost her balance and buckled to one knee. Heart racing, she pulled herself to her feet and stepped as fast as she dared across the uneven logs. The bridge swayed even more and creaked in a new way. She could see the other side of the river. Solid ground was only twenty feet away.

Trying to maintain her balance, she put one foot in front of the other and gripped the rope railing.

A louder creak filled the air. She caught a glimpse of the rushing water down below, dark and cold. The bridge went slack. And then she felt her body slipping backward and down. Her hand flailed, struggling to find something to hold on to.

She grasped only air as her body plunged into the depths of the freezing water.

FOUR

Zane grabbed hold of the rope remnants of the bridge as he drifted downstream. Clarence's body rammed into his and then floated away as the animal struggled to keep its head above water. He saw a flash of Heather's jacket, and then she disappeared beneath the freezing water. His heart squeezed tight, and he waited for her to resurface.

A bullet whizzed past his head. He switched focus to the men—boys, really, no more than teenagers—on the shoreline. The first boy grabbed the gun from the second one, probably not wanting to risk Zane being killed since the orders were for them to be taken in alive.

Zane let go of the piece of tattered bridge as the current pulled him along. There was no more sign of Heather.

Twice, the force of the water pushed him under.

The young men ran along the bank, keeping him in sight. Zane couldn't see Clarence anywhere, but hoped that the mule had managed to reach land—something Zane now needed to do for himself. He swam hard to get to the far bank. That bridge had been the only way across the water for miles. The young men on the shore slowed down as the current carried him along even faster.

Though he couldn't see her, he refused to believe Heather had drowned. She had proved she was a competent athlete.

He knew he had only minutes in the freezing water before hypothermia set in. The current pushed him back toward the closer shore where the pursuers were. He and Heather really needed to get across this river. He rounded a bend. The young men with guns grew smaller then disappeared from view. He felt a rush of relief when he saw Heather up ahead crawling up on a log that had fallen half way across the stream. She had almost reached land, but not on the far shore that would allow them to get back to town. If he followed her, they'd still be trapped on the wrong side of the river. All the same, he was elated to see she had made it out.

He swam through the water, trying to maneuver toward her. She noticed him and worked her way back to the end of the log and held out a hand. She grabbed him by the back of the collar as he drifted by. He angled his torso and braced himself with one of the heavier limbs on the fallen tree as water suctioned around him. She reached out an ice-cold hand and helped him up on the log.

Both of them were soaked and shivering, but at least they'd survived. She rose to her feet and edged her way across the slippery log to dry land. He was right behind her.

He glanced down the shoreline but saw no sign of their pursuers yet. Heather wrapped her arms around her body and waited for him. Water dripped from her long dark hair.

He surveyed the landscape. They'd drifted far enough that it would be a while before their pursuers caught up with them. He knew where he was and where they could go to get warm. "We need to build a fire, but not where we'll be seen easily."

"Where can we go?" Her eyes appeared glazed when she looked at him. Shock was setting in. Hypothermia couldn't be far behind.

He placed his palms on her cheeks, forcing her to make eye contact. "Just stay with me. Do what I say. I got this, okay?"

She nodded.

He sprinted through the trees up toward a rock face until he found an outcropping of rock that would provide shelter on three sides.

"Gather any dry wood you can find," he said.

One of the things he'd pulled off the saddlebags was a waterproof bag containing magnesium fire starter and dryer lint for kindling. As he drew the fire starter out of the plastic bag, he noticed that his whole body trembled.

Heather returned a few minutes later with a pile of sticks. "Everything is pretty wet." Her voice was shaky from the cold and all the color had drained from her face.

They needed to hurry and get this fire built.

"Anything you can find will help." He drew his knife off his belt. "I can split it. The wood on the inside is dry."

"I'll go find more." She turned and dashed toward the trees.

Using one log as a baton and his knife as a hatchet, he split several logs. His vision blurred as water dripped off his hair. He squeezed his eyes shut then opened them.

Dear God, help us stay alive.

He could feel the strength draining from his body and his mind fogging. Heather returned with more wood.

"I've got enough here to start the fire." He pointed at the fire starter. "Do you know how to use that?"

She nodded. "We go camping in California, too, you know."

She knelt down beside him, gathering the kindling into a pile around the dryer lint. She shaved off some magnesium flakes and then slid the scraper across the rod until she made some sparks. Her hands were shaking, too, as she used them to protect the fragile flames. Once the fire consumed the kindling, Zane placed larger pieces of wood on the fire until he could feel the warmth.

He slipped out of his wet coat. "You might want to take yours off. Lay it across those rocks so the fire will dry it out. You'll need to sit close to me…for warmth."

She gave him a momentary stare before stripping her coat and gloves off and scooting beside him.

"All right if I wrap my arms around you?"

She nodded. He took her into an awkward hug. Her body was rigid in his arms, unmoving except for the shivering. Both of them watched the flames as they warmed up and dried out.

"Will they come looking for us?" Her voice sounded very far away and weak.

He lifted his head to look around. Their would-be captors had been tenacious up to this point. There was no reason to think they would just give up now. "Probably." The fire was small, and they were hidden by the rocks, but they couldn't stay here for long without running the risk of being found.

"Who are they?"

Her question fell like a heavy weight on his chest. He took in a breath as the past rushed at him at a hundred miles an hour. This wasn't the first time she'd asked the question. He needed to finally give her an answer. "There's a man who used to live in these mountains. He's a doomsday-conspiracy kind of guy who thinks that the authorities are out to get him. So he lives out in places like this, in the middle of nowhere. He recruits boys and young men who need a father figure, indoctrinates them to be just as wild and lawless as he is. They're his own personal army, committing whatever crimes he plans. This area was his territory for a long time. He left almost seven years ago. He must be back here for some reason."

"How do you know it's him?"

"The way those boys acted. And then I heard them mention Willis's name," he said.

"How do you know all this about him and his boys?" She brushed a strand of wet hair off her neck.

He took a moment to answer. "I used to be one of them when I was a kid. I was just as wild, until I met your father."

The stiffness of her body against his softened a little. She took a moment to ask her next question. "My father helped you get away from this Willis guy?"

He nodded. Seven years ago, Willis had made the mistake of telling Zane he needed to get a job in town to bring in money. It was something Willis demanded of many of his followers whose loyalty he thought was without question. But Willis hadn't known that Zane would bond so deeply with the man who hired him. Stephan's love for God and His creation and unconditional love for Zane had been such a contrast to Willis's harsh world of punishment and rewards.

She seemed to relax even more in his embrace. "Why do they want you—or me, for that matter?"

"I don't know." He had cut all ties with Willis and anyone who knew the man or held similar views.

"Maybe they're looking to punish you because you didn't want to be with them anymore," she said.

"That was years ago. Willis is a little crazy, but he's also very calculating. The law was breathing down his neck when he left here. He wouldn't risk returning just for revenge." Something had drawn Willis back here.

She slipped from his embrace, stood up and moved closer to the fire. "So what do we do?"

"We need to get across that river so we can get to town, contact the authorities," he said. "There's another crossing ten miles down."

Her expression didn't change. She held her hands closer to the fire. "They'll be looking for us there, don't you think?"

"Probably. Willis knows these mountains better than I do." Though he didn't want to scare her, he couldn't lie to her.

"It's never easy, is it?" She crossed her arms over her body. "I just wanted to spread Stephan's ashes, do the right thing." She turned slightly away from him.

He wondered what she was thinking. She must be afraid, yet she hadn't fallen apart, and she hadn't blamed him for the violence she'd been dragged into.

"We're pretty well hidden here. Once we're dried

out, we'll put the fire out and wait until dusk. The darkness will provide us some cover."

She turned back toward him and nodded. Then she sat down beside him again, watching the glow of the fire. He kept thinking that she would cry or get angry with him, but she didn't. Brave woman.

"This fire saved us," she said.

"Yes, it did." He studied her profile as the firelight danced on her pale skin. This was way more than she had bargained for. "I'm sorry. When all this is over and done with, I'll take you back up to that mountain so you can do what you came here to do."

A faint smile crossed her lips and she nodded. But something in her expression suggested that she didn't believe him. Did she think they were going to die out here? "Was it really because of my father that you were able to leave Willis?"

"With Willis you were always scrambling for his approval, trying to accomplish things so he'd pat you on the back. Your father's love was filled with grace. His support gave me the strength I needed to get away from that life."

"I wish I could have known that Stephan." She shook her head, and her voice faltered. "I wish I could have known him at all. If he loved me, why didn't he try to get in touch with me when he was alive? I couldn't have been that hard to track down. His lawyer found me easily enough."

"Maybe he did try once he stopped drinking. Did your mom ever say anything to you about that?"

She shook her head. "Mom died a year ago, so I can't even ask her now."

He stood up beside her and touched her shoulder

lightly, knowing that there were no words that would take away her pain and confusion.

They waited until the light faded. Hunger gnawed at his belly as they headed back toward the river. He'd grabbed protein bars from the saddlebags. Since that was their only food, he didn't want to eat them until they had no calorie reserves left. They might be out here for a long time. He needed to be smart about when they ate their only food.

Behind him, Heather's footsteps stopped. He turned to face her, barely able to make out her features in the fading light.

"Something wrong?"

"Thought I heard something."

He studied the landscape, tuning his ears to the hum of the forest. He understood her jumpiness. He felt it too. Willis taught all his protégés tracking skills, so he had to assume that sooner or later they would encounter one or more of the followers who had been assigned to bring Heather and him in.

As he listened, nothing seemed amiss and nothing sounded human. Still, better safe than sorry.

He turned and headed back down the hill. He heard Heather's footsteps behind him but nothing else. The silence was unnerving as they moved through the forest.

A flood of memories of his time with Willis came back to him with each step he took. He's been barely seventeen when Willis had caught him breaking into his car to sleep. Jordan—Jordie—had only been thirteen when they decided a few months earlier that living on the run was better than foster care. His little brother had been even more impressionable than he had been.

So many of Willis's antiestablishment rants hadn't rang true or lacked a certain logic, but that was easy to overlook when Willis's ragtag community finally gave Zane a place where he felt like he belonged. It was the pats on the back and the way Willis would take the time with him to teach him to shoot, build a lean-to and hunt that had made him want to stay in the wild. The camaraderie with the other boys and men filled a void for him, too. It had been hard to leave that behind, even when he'd known it was the right thing to do. The hardest part had been parting from Jordie, who'd refused to leave with him.

His brother would be twenty now, a man. Jordan had gone with Willis and the others when they left the area, but had he stayed with him all these years?

Zane stuttered in his step. Heather came up close to him. Her shoulder pressed against his as he heard her sharp intake of breath. To the east, the river murmured.

Though he heard nothing amiss, his heart beat a little faster. "You hear something?"

After a moment, she shook her head. "I guess not. I'm just a little nervous."

His warning system was on high alert as well. Now that they were out in the open, he had to assume they were being tracked.

"Stay close," he whispered.

He moved slower, choosing each step with a degree of caution, not wanting a single sound to alert anyone tracking them to their location. Heather seemed to instinctually know that she needed to be quiet. Her steps were almost lighter than air.

A wolf howled somewhere in the distance. Zane's heart hammered out a steady beat. He pushed through trees, seeking more cover. The gray dusk light turned charcoal. Stars glimmered above them, but he could not take the time to notice their beauty. He dared not let himself relax or let his guard down.

"I'm thirsty," whispered Heather as she came up beside him.

She was probably hungry, too.

He just wasn't sure if stopping to eat the protein bars was a good idea right now. "Don't eat the snow. We'll drink from the river."

He followed the sound of the water rushing over stones. He crouched low and chose a sheltered spot where the cottonwoods grew close to the water.

Heather knelt beside the river.

"It's cold. Drink just enough to keep you going. I have food. We'll eat in a while."

He positioned himself beside her and cupped his own hands and placed them in the icy water. After several handfuls, he stood up and tugged on Heather's coat. She rose to her feet and they slipped back into the shelter of the forest.

The canopy of the trees and the encroaching darkness made it hard to see. He heard a yelp that was clearly human off to his side, maybe ten feet away. He grabbed Heather's hand and pulled her to the ground.

Both of them remained still as the footfalls of a human being overwhelmed the other forest sounds. Heavy boots pounded past them.

One guy alone. Zane should be able to take him and get a weapon. Zane leaped to his feet and jumped on the teenager. The young man turned out to be the size of a football player and with the same strength. They wrestled, crashing against the brush. The teenager flipped over on his stomach in an effort to push himself to his feet.

The shouts of the other boys filled the forest. Their position had been given away by the noise of the fight, and reinforcements were closing in.

Zane kept a knee in Football Player's back as he felt along his waistband for a gun. He retrieved a small pistol.

Now the whole forest was full of the noise of their pursuers edging closer. He saw bobbing lights. The mechanical thunder of ATVs coming to life surrounded them.

Heather pulled on his shoulder. "Hurry. They're coming."

She let go of him and turned to head away from the bobbing lights. He stuffed the gun in his waistband and took a step toward her. From the ground where he lay, Football Player grabbed at his ankle. Zane stumbled, nearly falling on his face.

Heather swung around and landed a kick to the kid's shoulder so he let go of Zane's foot. The crashing and breaking of branches alerted them to the closeness of their pursuers. They shot through forest and back up toward a sloping hill. The roar of ATVs pressed on them from all sides. When he glanced over his shoulder, he saw three sets of glowing white headlights. They'd never outrun these machines.

He rerouted toward a cluster of trees. Heather followed him. Once they were deep into the forest, he stopped.

He pointed at a tree. "Climb."

Heather must have realized hiding was their only option. Without a word, she dashed toward the tree and grabbed a low, sturdy branch. She climbed with agility and ease. He ran to a nearby tree and jumped up to grasp one of the lower branches. The ATVs grew louder. Headlights cut a wide swath through the trees. As artificial light filled the forest, he could make out the silhouette of Heather resting her belly on a stout branch and holding on to the smaller limbs of the tree. Evergreen boughs partially hid her, but wouldn't provide enough protection if someone looked her way. He could only hope their pursuers kept their eyes on the ground.

The machines surged by beneath them. He spotted two riders by themselves. A third ATV with a driver and a passenger zoomed by. The ATVs scooted up the hill, the noise of their engines growing faint. The bobbing flashlights told him there were some trackers on foot, as well. These searchers approached at a slower pace, shining their light over the brush and trees. The orange glow of the flashlights landed on the tree where Heather was hiding. Zane tensed. If they were spotted, they'd be shot like coons out of their trees even if it was just to injure them.

In the distance, the ATVs slowed. They must have figured out they'd lost the trail and now they were backtracking. There were three young men with flashlights on foot. One of them lingered beneath the tree where Heather was hiding.

He'd counted seven boys and young men chasing after them in all. As far as he could tell in the dark, none of them were Jordie. Though the passing of time would make it hard to recognize his brother even in daylight. He could only hope that his brother had escaped the control Willis had had on his life.

The lone searcher continued to pace beneath Heather's hiding place, shining the flashlight on nearby trees. Zane could no longer hear the noise of the other two foot soldiers who had split off and disappeared into the forest.

Zane clenched his teeth. All they needed was for this tracker to leave, and they could scramble down and find a new hiding place or even escape.

It sounded like the ATVs were doing circles, trying to pick up the trail. The man shone his light on the tree where Zane hid. The light glared in Zane's face. He'd been spotted. Zane's muscles tensed as the man reached for his gun.

FIVE

Zane jumped down from his hiding place and pounced on the man, knocking the wind out of him. Zane grabbed the flashlight where it had rolled away from the temporarily disabled man. By then, Heather was halfway down the tree. She ran the remaining ten feet to rush to his side.

Between the two other searchers on foot and the ATVs coming back this way, there was only one direction to go. Both of them took off running. Zane led them in an erratic path around the trees, hoping to make them harder to follow.

He caught glimpses of bobbing lights in the forest. They needed to shake these guys before they had any chance of getting back to the river.

He pushed deeper into the forest where the undergrowth was thick. The roar of the ATVs never let up. They skirted around some brush, coming face-to-face with a kid on foot who didn't look to be more than twelve years old. When he saw them, the kid's eyes grew wide with fear. He showed no sign of pulling any kind of a weapon on them.

"I won't tell if you don't," said Zane as he darted off in a different direction with Heather close on his heels.

They sprinted through the darkness of the forest, dodging lights and sounds that seemed to come at them from every direction, feet pounding the ground, breath filling their lungs and coming out in cloudy puffs as the night grew colder.

He dismissed any thought of returning to the river just yet. The river was probably patrolled anyway.

They ran until twenty minutes passed without seeing a light or hearing a human noise. Both of them pressed against tree trunks in an aspen grove, the sounds of their heavy inhales and exhales the only noise around.

They couldn't keep dodging these guys forever. Granted, it looked like Willis had sent the B team, younger men and boys with less high-tech equipment and experience, to track them down, but if Willis was serious about kidnapping Zane and Heather, he'd send the A team or come out himself sooner or later.

Heather pushed off the tree and moved toward him as if to talk to him.

In his peripheral vision, he saw the vapor cloud of someone exhaling by a tree. His heart skipped a beat as he held up his hand, indicating to Heather she needed to stand still.

He watched as the person behind the tree let out another breath from maybe twenty feet away.

Seconds ticked by.

Though her face was covered in shadows, he picked up on the fear in Heather's posture. Both of them stood as still as rocks. His heartbeat drummed in his ears.

Whoever was behind the tree took a single step, feet crunching on snow.

Heather turned her head ever so slightly as if to indicate that she thought they should run. He shook his head. He didn't think they'd been spotted yet, but any noise at all would alert the stranger to their whereabouts.

The stranger took another step. Through the prism of the narrow white and black aspen trunks, Zane discerned the silhouette of a man, standing still for a long time as though he were taking in his surroundings. Probably listening for any noise that might be out of place.

Zane swallowed as his heart raged in his chest and sweat trickled down his back. His mouth was dry.

With the next footstep, the stranger moved away from where he and Heather stood. The footsteps came one after the other before finally fading into the distance.

When the man got far enough away that they could no longer hear him, Heather let out a breath, and her shoulders slumped, but she didn't move until Zane took a step toward her.

She closed the distance between them so she could talk in a whisper. "Who was that?"

"I'm not sure," he said.

Another hunter? Maybe. More likely it was someone in Willis's crew who was out in the woods for some reason other than capturing them. Or someone who was supposed to catch them but who didn't want to get into a wrestling match.

Zane ran his hand over the pistol he'd gotten off the teenager, grateful that he hadn't needed to use it.

"Follow me," he said.

They walked for a distance through the darkness. It was too much of a risk to turn on the flashlight, and the moonlight provided enough light to see the ground. He stopped at the top of a knoll and stared down at the cluster of trees below. He turned the flashlight on and off just to get a glimpse. Something about the arrangement of the underbrush looked unnatural.

Heather followed him down the hill and into the evergreens. Hidden from view from the outside, he saw piles of pine boughs covering some sort of structure. He pulled several of the branches off until he found a small door. The structure was made of heavy duty plastic stretched across PVC pipe and it was not more than four feet high.

"It's like a hobbit house," said Heather.

He poked his head in. A gust of warmth surrounded him. "Actually, it's a little more sinister than that." He pulled out the flashlight and turned it on. As he'd suspected, they'd stumbled on someone's pot farm. "Might as well come in, it's warm inside."

The plants were spaced to allow a single person to get around to tend them. Heather slipped in after him. "Someone has a serious need to support a habit."

"This kind of operation isn't about personal use. Someone is growing this stuff to sell."

And from the look of the empty shelves, much of it already had been sold. He'd received letters from law enforcement telling him to be on the lookout for the pot farms in the high country because it was such a good place to hide an operation. As much time as he spent up here, he was bound to stumble across one sooner or later. He wondered, too, if the stranger they'd encoun-

tered in the woods had just left the little hidden farm.
Maybe he was part of Willis's group but spent most
of his time away from the main base and had no idea
about Zane and Heather being hunted by the others.
An operation like this required daily attention. From
the size of the plants, they'd been up here for a while.
With the limited number of people who came up here
outside of hunting season, Willis might have been here
through the spring and summer.

"I guess they're not likely to get caught this far away
from everyone." Heather scooted in behind him and
closed the tiny door.

"Right." The more he thought about it, the more certain Zane was that no one besides Willis and his little
army would be this far up. The little farm had to be
Willis's. Willis had always been against the consump-
tion of drugs and alcohol, but he wasn't above selling it
to others to make money. This was a larger crop than
Zane would have expected, though. What exactly was
Willis up to anyway? What was he trying to finance?

Once hunting season started in a few weeks, Willis
ran the risk of being spotted, so it must be something
that would happen soon.

Zane shone his flashlight around, spotting a pamph-
let that was authored by Willis. Any doubt that this
operation was his fell away. Zane noticed a water container. He lifted it and handed it first to Heather. She
took several gulps of water as he skirted around the
dirt floor to see what else he could find. He came up
with a blanket neatly folded and a heavy-duty sleeping
bag on a mat.

"There's a little stove here and some canned goods."

He heard Heather's voice but couldn't see her through the foliage.

When he studied the roof, it looked like there was some sort of solar panel set up to keep the place warm. Whoever tended the plants must stay here for extended periods. No doubt he would be back. But hopefully not before Zane and Heather had a chance to take refuge for a little while.

He worked his way over to where Heather had already fired up the little propane stove and was opening a can of beans.

He patted the protein bars in his pocket, grateful he could save them for later. "Let's eat and get out of here. I'm sure someone checks these on a regular basis. The 'farmer' might be the guy we saw a few minutes ago, just out for a brief walk."

Heather poured the beans into the metal tin and placed it on the gas flame.

He felt a sense of urgency. "Maybe we should eat the beans cold."

She cut the flame. "There's only one spoon."

"You first," he said.

She took four quick bites and then handed him the can. He'd finished his third bite when he heard the roar of the ATVs raging down the hill toward them. So much for rest and food. They'd been found again. Time to run.

Bright lights glaring through the clear plastic nearly paralyzed Heather. Zane clicked off the flashlight. She heard him scrambling toward the door. It took her a moment before her brain kicked into gear, and she followed behind him, slipping through the tiny opening and out into the dark night.

The ATVs loomed down the hill toward them, the engine noises sounding like hungry monsters gnashing their teeth. Her limbs felt heavy and muscles cried out with fatigue from having run so much.

Zane grabbed her hand and pulled her toward the shelter of the trees. The ATV noise fell away by half, indicating some of their pursuers must have stopped to examine the greenhouse. She kept her eyes on the back of Zane's head as they fled. They ran until the noise died down to a single ATV and then fell away altogether.

When the silence of the forest surrounded them once again, they ran and rested and ran some more until the sun peeked up over the mountains. Early-morning light washed everything with a warm glow, and she felt her strength returning.

They stopped only briefly to eat the protein bars Zane had gotten from Clarence's saddlebag.

It seemed to her that they'd been running in circles, but she knew Zane was smarter than that, and knew the area well enough to be choosing their direction carefully. He must be trying to figure out a safe way to get down off the mountain, back to the river and back to Fort Madison.

The landscape opened up to flat meadow that was partially covered in snow. She shaded her eyes from the glare. In the distance, she spotted a red and blue object that looked out of place.

She ran toward it. As she drew closer, more colors became evident. It was a backpack. She knelt down.

The backpack was empty. Another hiker who had been robbed maybe?

Zane knelt beside her. He bolted to his feet and glanced around.

Heather stood up, too, studying the partially snowy landscape. She spotted a yellow object attached to the branch of a tree and ran toward it. She pulled the fabric free of the branches, her chest tightening. The fabric was from a man's bandanna.

She glanced up just as Zane disappeared into another part of the forest. Her feet pounded the earth as she followed after him, stepping through patches of crunchy snow and into the trees. The canopy of evergreens cut the light by half as she stepped deeper into the forest. Her breath caught when she glanced down at the ground. Dribbles and several huge circles of dried blood spotted the snow.

Her chest felt like it was in a vice. She tried to tell herself that the blood could be from an animal—but there had been no sign of teeth or claw marks on the belongings they'd spotted. The backpack and bandanna looked like they'd been discarded by human hands.

Zane burst through the trees. His expression was like none she'd ever witnessed before. Eyebrows knit in anguish, his skin the color of rice. Eyes filled with fear. He glanced over his shoulder and then back at her.

"What is it?" She stepped toward where he'd looked.

He grabbed her arm at the elbow. "You don't need to see this."

She pulled away, not able to let go of the idea that she had to know what was going on in these mountains. She darted toward where Zane had come from.

She found the man's body propped up against the

tree. The body had not started to decompose, so he must have been here a short time. The bloodstain on his chest revealed that he had been stabbed.

Light-headed, she whirled away, slamming into Zane's chest. He wrapped his arms around her and pulled her away from the gruesome sight.

Her mind reeled. *Murderers.* She'd been so focused on running for her life that reality hadn't sunk in until she saw the dead man. They were trapped on this mountain with bloodthirsty killers.

She rested for a moment in the security of Zane's arms, trying to calm herself. But her mind raced at a thousand miles an hour. She fought to get a deep breath.

She could barely get the words out. "What happened...there? Did they kill him so they could get his stuff?" She pulled away from him, then paced back and forth gripping her somersaulting stomach. "Do they have so little regard for life?"

He stepped toward her. "Calm down."

"Calm down?" Her words splintered as they spilled from her lips. Her legs felt like were made of rubber. She'd only come up here to spread her father's ashes. How had things gotten to this point where she was fighting to get away from men who acted worse than animals?

He reached out for her.

She darted away, shaking her head. "What is going on here?"

"Heather, please." He stepped toward her.

"You knew these men. You were one of them." Really, if Zane hadn't told her that he used to be under the influence of someone like Willis, she never would have guessed it. Was it really possible a man could change so radically?

"I am nothing like them." Zane's voice was tinged with anger. "Not anymore. And this is way over the top. We never did anything like that when I was with Willis."

"It looks like they are getting more desperate or bloodthirsty, then. What is driving them?" Her voice was barely above a whisper. Her mind clouded as a fear she had never felt before invaded her awareness. She turned nearly a full circle. The killers were out there waiting to attack again, looking for the chance to take her and Zane. But after they used them for whatever they had in mind, would she and Zane die, too?

"Heather, please don't give up." He stepped toward her and cupped his hands on her shoulders. "We need to get back to town so the authorities can come up here and deal with these men."

She nodded slowly. He was right. They could not stop fighting or give in to fear.

Zane took a step back from her. "I'm going to check to see if there's any ID on that man. His family deserves to have closure." His voice was filled with compassion. "There have been no reports of missing hikers that I've seen. He couldn't have been up here for long. The family might not expect him back for weeks. You don't need to come with me. Just stay right here."

She closed her eyes and turned away, unable to get the image of the dead man out of her head. She crossed her arms over her chest and paced in a huge circle, trying to wipe the picture from her brain.

She pushed aside the despair that threatened to pull her into a dark place. She stared up at the blue sky, where snowflakes were drifting down. A memory that had been long buried floated to the surface of her mind. She was outside a cabin with her father, laughing as they caught snowflakes on their tongues. How strange that she hadn't remembered that until now. The memory comforted her at a time when anxiety threatened to rule her.

A rustling to the side of her caught her attention. She turned, expecting to see Zane. A man came at her so suddenly that there was no chance for her to scream or fight. She didn't even have time to register what he looked like before she was knocked to the ground and a hood was put over her head.

Zane put the ID he'd found of the man in his pocket, pausing a moment to say a prayer for the family. His thoughts were interrupted as the engine noise of the ATVs filled the forest.

The pursuers had found them. He needed to get to Heather and fast.

He dare not call out and give away his position. He saw flashes of color and motion through the trees, then he caught a glimpse of a man pointing in his direction. He'd been spotted.

He was able to guess at where Heather had been when a patch of snow revealed her boot print. But where was she now?

Two armed men surged through the trees. Zane slipped behind some brush before they had a chance to get a shot off. He burst up from his hiding place as they drew near. He sprinted, hoping to lose the men in the labyrinth of the forest. The noise behind him increased. More men must have fallen in with the two he'd seen. He had to find a way to shake them so he could circle back and get to Heather.

His heart beat hard in his chest as he ran from one hiding place to the next. The sound of the men yelling commands at each other fell on his ears. They were closing in on him from all sides.

He ran toward higher ground, pushing past a rocky mountainside. When he glanced over his shoulder, he spotted men and ATVs snaking through the trees, converging around him.

Where was Heather? Had she been smart enough to find a hiding place that their pursuers hadn't spotted? It didn't seem likely—these men were carefully trained, and Heather lacked their knowledge of the area. So why hadn't he heard or seen her running, too? He scanned the landscape, not seeing her anywhere.

Three of them men on foot closed in on him, making quick progress up the steep hillside.

Zane dived behind a large boulder and lined up a shot with his pistol. He fired three shots in quick succession. The men gaining ground on him fell flat to the ground to avoid his gunfire.

Zane hurried farther up the hillside before the men had time to recover. If they did want him alive, they'd be cautious about shooting at him, which gave him a slight advantage as long as they were at a distance. But he couldn't let them get close enough to grab him. It was essential that he widen the gap between them, even as his leg muscles strained on the steep incline.

He glanced over his shoulder. The ATVs had slowed, and the men on foot were losing enthusiasm as well. Zane hurried up the remainder of the incline until he reached a high point that allowed him a view of much of the valley below. The ATVs still traversed the countryside but the infantry must have given up for now. The men on the machines would only be able to get so far up the hill before they'd have to get off and walk.

He spotted some ATVs headed away from him. He squinted to make out details. His chest squeezed tight when he recognized Heather's pink gloves, which stood out from her camo outfit. She had a hood over her head.

Heart racing, he jumped from the rock where he'd been perched. He watched the direction the vehicles were headed. Willis must have a camp farther up the mountain than the base Zane remembered. It would take him hours to track them on foot but he had to try.

Aware that the hills were probably still crawling with pursuers trying to earn their stripes, he moved across the terrain on full alert.

The thought of anything bad happening to Heather made him run even faster.

He heard the distant clang of an ATV. He glanced through the trees down the hillside. One machine off by itself, one rider. He could take him and get the transport he needed.

Zane ran out into the open where the ATV rider would see him. The rider turned in an arc and headed toward Zane, kicking up dirt with his wheels. Using himself as bait was risky, but it was the only way to lure the rider and get the machine.

Zane studied the landscape for a good ambush spot and hurried toward it. The noise of the ATV grew louder in his ears as he pressed on toward the high point where he could hide. The trick was to be seen enough so the rider wouldn't give up, but to hide without him knowing it. He was able to slip out of view of the rider.

Though he could not see the machine, he could hear it. The echo off the mountains made it hard to track exactly where his pursuer was. He pushed through to an open area just as rider and vehicle came into view. This was not going as planned. He'd hoped to be hiding and ambush the man. The man twisted the throttle and made a beeline for Zane.

Zane stumbled. The machine sounded like it was on top of him as he struggled to get to his feet. He could hear the engine idling as hands grabbed the back of his coat collar.

This was not a kid. He was dealing with a full-grown man. Zane spun around, but the man was able to land the first blow across his jaw.

With his face stinging from the impact, Zane swung hard with a left then a right, knocking the man on the ground.

He knew this man from seven years ago. His name was John. He'd been just a kid then, like Zane. Now his face looked leathery and weathered, and he was clearly a seasoned fighter. John jumped to his feet and reached out toward Zane.

Zane dodged the intended blow and hit the other man twice in the stomach. His opponent doubled over. Zane ran toward the idling ATV and jumped on, revving it and shifting into gear. He took off with a jerk—but he wasn't quite fast enough to evade John, who managed to grab hold of the back of Zane's shirt.

Zane felt his collar pull tight as he increased speed. Zane shifted into a higher gear, still struggling for breath. The pressure on his neck let up.

He shifted again and headed up the makeshift trail, looking for the ATV tracks that would lead him to the camp. When he glanced over his shoulder, John was just getting to his feet. At least he'd lost that guy, but it didn't mean he was in the clear.

The members of Willis's cult used radios to communicate. It would probably be just a matter of minutes before another pursuer zeroed in on Zane's location. He thought about taking a more roundabout route to where the camp might be, but time was precious if he was going to get Heather out of danger. He could not spare the minutes a detour would cost him.

He sped up. The terrain was more overgrown than he remembered it. This wasn't a part of the mountain where he took hunters, which made it a high probability for Willis's camp. He pushed aside any thought of something bad happening to Heather. Thinking the worst could cripple him mentally. He needed to focus on what needed to be done. He had to assume she had not been harmed and that he'd be able to free her.

He knew, though, that the challenges were growing. Willis had started sending his more experienced and older men. That meant he was upping his game, and it meant he saw Zane as more of a threat than he'd predicted. If Heather was taken to camp, Willis would know to keep her well guarded. Getting her out wouldn't be easy.

He'd cross that bridge when he came to it.

Zane pushed the ATV through the thick undergrowth and across bumpy open areas. He rode until he saw smoke rising off in the distance. That had to be the camp. Reluctantly, he got off the ATV, taking the time to cover it with branches. He would be more likely to avoid detection if he moved in on foot. With God's help, he'd be able to free Heather and come back to the ATV to make a quick escape.

That was the plan anyway. He prayed that everything would fall into place and they both wouldn't end up dead at the hands of Willis's men.

SIX

Heather struggled to take in a deep breath as the fabric of the hood pressed against her face with each intake of air. She couldn't adjust the position of the hood—not with the way her wrists had been bound with rope in front of her. Finally, the jostling on the back of the ATV ceased. The engine clicked off and the rider dismounted.

She shivered involuntarily, listening to the noise around her. She heard footsteps close by and whispering farther away, a conversation that sounded urgent even though it was hushed.

Then she heard the distinct noise of a 12-gauge shotgun being ratcheted back and forth, the lethal cartridge sliding into the chamber.

Her back stiffened and her breath caught like a bubble in her throat. For a long moment, all she heard was the pulsing of her own heartbeat. She squeezed her eyes shut.

Dear God, if they are going to shoot me, let it happen quickly. Don't draw this thing out.

The prayer caught her by surprise. She hadn't prayed to God with such intensity since she was a little girl, on the day her mother had loaded her into the car and pulled out of the gravel driveway, leaving behind Stephan and their life as a family forever. The memory had been buried all these years. But now the image of her father standing in the driveway as she looked out the back window burned through her mind. That had been a sort of death, too.

Several footsteps crunched through the snow, jerking her out of the emotions and images of the past.

"What are you doing?" said a male voice off to her side. His voice was filled with accusation.

She turned her head in the direction of the voice, wondering if he was talking to her.

"I was just having some fun. What good is she without the guy anyway?" said the second voice.

"We *will* catch Zane." The first voice sounded as though his teeth were gritted. "Now put the shotgun away. She'll be useful to us anyway."

Heather let out a gust of air. She'd be spared...for now. Though the word *useful* sent chills down her spine. She'd seen how violent these men and boys could be. What did they have in store for her?

The conversation between the two men was clear enough that she was able to pick up pieces of the exchange. She learned that Zane was still out there and that Heather had been blindfolded from the start so she would have no idea where the camp was located. The older-sounding man who had stayed her execution seemed to be in charge. Was this the man Zane had told her about?

The camp fell silent again. She suspected the two men had wandered away. She could hear other sounds, muffled whispers and even laughter and the crackle of a campfire some distance from her.

Footsteps approached her. She sensed someone close just before the hood was yanked from her head. She'd guess that the man in front of her was maybe twenty years of age, though it was hard to tell because all these men clearly spent most of their life out battling the elements.

He leaned close to her, and she bristled. He was in desperate need of a shower. His hair was past his shoulders, and his beard hit his chest. She couldn't distinguish much more about his features because of the profuse amount of facial hair.

"Get off of there," he said. The voice was the same as the man who had stayed her execution.

Dismounting the ATV was a bit of a balancing challenge with her arms tied in front of her. The man held out a hand and steadied her by cupping her elbow. The gesture seemed out of character for a man who appeared so uncivilized.

She scanned the area without turning her neck so he wouldn't realize she was taking in her surroundings. Why risk getting the hood put back on her head? Three tents placed close together stood not too far from a campfire. She could make out the shadowed figures of men as they stood back from the flames. One of the men stepped closer to the fire, revealing a sneering face.

Her chest clamped tight. Though she could only see one man overtly leering at her, she could feel eyes on her, taking her apart.

Had it been God's mercy to spare her life or was she about to face a violence she might not ever forget? The man with the long hair pointed toward the center tent.

"Go in there." He lifted his chin at one of the men loitering around the fire. "Get some grub for her."

At least they were going to feed her. Maybe that was a good sign. Though her stomach was clenched so tight she doubted she'd be able to keep any food down. She stepped into the tent.

"Sit down," the man with the long hair commanded.

She settled down on an animal skin. Several other animal skins, a sleeping bag and a crossbow populated the rest of the space. The man with the long hair never took his eyes off her, which only fed her anxious thoughts.

She swallowed, trying to produce some moisture in her mouth.

The man grinned at her. "Relax, you're okay for now." His voice seemed genuine, not menacing.

A younger man poked his head in the tent, holding a piece of wood that contained piles of food. "Here, sir."

The long-haired man took the makeshift plate. He sat it beside Heather, then used a knife to cut Heather's hands free.

"Eat up," he said.

She stared down at the food, which looked to be some kind of cooked red meat. She didn't see a fork. She lifted the first morsel and put in in her mouth. The meat was surprisingly tender and almost sweet tasting.

The long-haired man switched his knife from one hand to the other. The silver of the blade picked up glints of light. His actions made it clear that if she tried to escape, he wouldn't hesitate to use the knife.

"You like it?" He pointed at the meat with his knife.

She nodded. As famished as she was, she would

have eaten almost anything, but the meat genuinely was good.

"It's elk," he said. "We hunt it year-round. That's part of the privilege of living up here. We're not beholden to the government's restrictive hunting regulations."

She made a tactical choice not to respond to the ideology that drove his statement. "I've never tasted elk before." Even as she spoke, an unexpected memory floated back into her mind. Her father had prepared a similar meal for her. She could see the rough-hewn logs of the cabin where they'd lived and smell the wood burning in the fireplace. The memories all seemed faint and far away, but real all the same.

Maybe that was why her father had wanted her to come back here. Being in these mountains brought images of her childhood to the surface that her mother's bitterness had buried. She hadn't even realized the memories were there. "I've had deer meat. My father used to prepare it for me."

She took several more bites of the meat. The long-haired man never took his eyes off her.

She lowered her head and looked away. "I'm sorry. Guess I'm eating kind of fast. I'm just really hungry."

The man waved her rudeness away with his hand. "Eat up. There's plenty." He leaned back on his elbows and continued to watch her.

She stopped chewing the meat and studied the man in front of her. His expression was hard to read with the thick beard. His eyes were cold, but he had not been cruel or menacing to her in any way. Was that just as act? What kind of game was he playing anyway? Was he the one who killed the man they'd found in the forest?

The long-haired man sat back up. He stared off to the side and resumed playing with his knife. "So why did you come up here with Zane?"

It seemed a strange question to ask. "Why do you want to know?" The way he said Zane's name, as though he were spitting it out of his mouth, made her think there was some kind of history between the two men.

The man shrugged. "In order to find out."

She concluded that the less he knew about her, the better. "Are you Willis?" A chill ran down her back when she said the name. Though it was hard to judge the man's age, she'd assumed Willis would be older.

The man threw back his head and laughed. "You have no idea." He rose to his feet, grabbed the crossbow and slipped out of the tent.

After a few minutes passed, she placed the wooden plate to one side and peered out of the tent. He wouldn't have left her untied unless he knew there was no way for her to escape. All the same, she had to assess her chances. She counted five men milling around the fire and suspected there might be one or two more in the other tents. Everyone she could see carried a knife or gun on their belts.

She checked her own jeans for the pocketknife she'd used to cut Zane free, but it was nowhere to be found. She must have dropped it in the panic to get away.

She continued to watch the camp. The long-haired man barked orders at the others, and they scattered into the trees. Then he stalked back toward her tent. Heather slipped inside and put the plate back on her lap.

The man stuck his head into the tent. "Get some rest. I'll be back for you in a few hours."

Her mind raced as dark images seemed to assault her at every turn. What did he have planned? Whatever these men had in mind, it sounded like their plan wouldn't work without Zane. The long-haired man had probably ordered the others to go capture Zane.

She was pretty sure she was too anxious to sleep despite having been up for more than twenty-four hours. All the same, she laid her head down on the animal skin and closed her eyes. The fog of sleep overtook her slowly as her thoughts tumbled one over the other...

"Get up."

Someone shook her shoulder. Her eyes fluttered open. How long had she been asleep?

The long-haired man loomed above her. "Time to go, sweetheart."

Through the open tent door, she saw the sky was still light. She'd slept for a few hours at least.

He stepped back to let her through the tent flap. "Hurry it up."

She crawled out and got up on her feet. She thought to bolt for the forest, but his hand clamped around her arm so quickly she didn't have time. He pointed toward a cluster of trees. "Over there," he ordered several young men. "Get out of sight. It needs to look low security."

One of the young men stopped. "What are you doing with her?"

"She's bait for the real prize," said the long-haired man.

The answer sent chills through Heather, but she didn't argue or protest. She simply followed the man,

Big Sky Showdown

obeying when he indicated she needed to sit on the ground.

He gave her no opportunity for escape, tying her wrists together again before shouting toward the tents, "Tyler, bring me more rope."

A moment later, a teenager emerged from the shadows and dropped rope at the man's feet.

"Scoot up against that tree," he said.

"Zane isn't stupid. He won't fall for this." Her voice wavered with fear as she struggled to take in a deep breath.

The man ran a strand of rope around Heather and the tree. "The one thing I know about Zane is that his overdeveloped need to rescue the innocent will always trump his common sense."

So he did know Zane.

He stood up and peered off into the distance, frowning before returning his focus to her. "To answer your earlier question. No, my dear, I am not Willis. I'm Jordan. My friends call me Jordie." He leaned a little closer to her, brown eyes flashing with intensity. "You may call me Jordan."

Heather watched the dark trees, knowing that men were lying in wait to grab Zane and then...what, kill her?

"Making some kind of plan, are you?" Jordan leaned close to her. He pulled a scarf off his neck and reached to put it around her eyes.

She jerked her head away.

He grabbed her chin and squeezed it between his fingers. "Don't you dare resist me."

His voice struck a note of fear inside her. Clearly he was a man capable of violence.

The rope around her wrists had very little give. Her shoulders pressed against the tree trunk, not allowing for much movement there either. Though she could see only a few men milling around the camp, busy with their own tasks and seemingly paying little attention to her and Jordan, she had to assume she was being watched. There was little to no chance she would be able to escape on her own.

Jordan was wrong, though. Zane was smart. He wouldn't walk into a trap no matter how much responsibility he felt for her life.

As she listened to the sounds of the forest all around her, she prayed that Zane would be able to come up with a plan that would save them both rather than trying to rescue her and having them both end up dead.

Zane spotted the smoke rising up from a campfire above the trees just as the sky started to turn gray. He was certain it came from Willis's camp. This part of the mountains was remote and rugged. Most hunters didn't even come up this way. Willis could run his crazy operation completely undetected.

Darting from tree to tree, Zane approached the camp until the tents came into view. No one was gathered around the fire. Suspicious. He saw shadows and movement inside one of the tents.

He crawled a little closer. Heather was tied to a tree away from the camp. He breathed a sigh of relief that she was still alive. No guard stood close to her. This had to be a trap. Otherwise, they would have posted at least one guard close to her.

He studied the landscape, open areas and thick forest. Shooters were probably positioned at strategic high points. No doubt other men perched behind trees waiting for the chance to jump him. If he simply blundered into camp, they would both be prisoners.

He needed to create some sort of diversion. Something that would give him a few minutes—just a few, precious minutes—where he could swoop in and cut Heather loose.

He moved in a little closer, crouching low and using the brush for cover. He doubted Willis was close. The man tended to give orders from a safe distance. Zane watched the camp for a long time. Movement inside the tent stopped. A light went out.

Time was on his side. The men who'd been put on watch would grow weary of waiting for him to show up. They'd become distracted and less attentive.

From his vantage point, he could watch Heather. It pained him to see her tied up. She was probably afraid and maybe even cold. Had she been given anything to eat? Water? A place to rest? How much had she already had to endure just because she'd been in the wrong place at the wrong time?

It wasn't just that he felt responsible for what she was going through. He cared about her. The thought of any harm coming to her made it hard for him to breath.

He would break her free or die trying.

He waited and watched as the sky grew even darker. No one came back toward the dying fire, though he detected sounds deeper in the woods that were probably caused by humans. He spotted a propane can used to power a cookstove.

Now he saw his opportunity for a distraction. Nothing like a fire to set men into a panic. He moved past the back of the tent where he would guess the men slept. Even the cracking of his knees as he crept along made him cringe. He stopped and took in a breath.

Inside the tent, he heard the rustling of a sleeping bag. Zane held still for a long moment until the man quieted again. He reached for the propane and worked his way back toward the fire but stayed hidden in the shadows while he tore fabric from his flannel shirt and saturated it with propane. He wrapped the fabric around a stick and shoved it toward the fire. The fire crackled and flamed up as his torch caught on fire.

He had only seconds to act. He poured the remaining propane on the fire. It flared. He ran toward the tent and touched his torch to it and then to the second tent, as well. He tossed the torch in the direction of the third tent and then yelled, "Fire!" They'd be able to put the fire out quickly. He didn't want anyone to be harmed, only panicked and distracted. He dived into the shadows.

It took only seconds for the men in the tent to exit and start shouting for help. Zane slipped farther back into the shadows and made his way toward Heather, pulling his knife from the sheath.

He listened as the ruckus grew louder. Timing was everything. He waited only feet away from Heather for the men watching her to emerge from the trees and race toward the fire.

Three men appeared at intervals and dashed toward the fire. Was that all of them? He couldn't be sure—but he also knew he couldn't wait any longer. The distraction would only work for a short time.

Zane hurried toward Heather and cut her free. She pulled the blindfold off her eyes. Without a word, they both jumped to their feet and headed into the trees. The crashing behind them told him the men had figured out they'd been hoodwinked.

He grabbed Heather's hand and pulled, indicating that they needed to change direction. They were running in a predictable pattern, which made them too easy to track. She followed as he led. They charged through the forest, circling around to the backside of the camp. Staying close to the camp was risky but it was a move the pursuers wouldn't figure out right away.

The noise of their pursuers grew dimmer and more spread out. Heather and Zane skirted close to the smoldering tent where only one boy stomped on the flames and then sprinkled a canteen of water on it.

Zane's heart pounded against his ribs. Heather's heavy intake of breath told him she was on high alert, as well. He slipped behind a pile of elk and deer bones. Heather pressed in close to him.

He heard the baying of a dog. He tensed. The dog would be able to track them back to the camp faster than people would. He tugged on Heather's sleeve and tilted his head. She nodded in understanding.

They ran in the opposite direction the men had gone until they were some distance from the light of the camp. The barking of the dog grew louder and more intense as he sprinted. Heather's footsteps sounded behind him.

The dog sounded like he was on their heels. When he peered over his shoulder, he saw the men.

Heather caught up with him. Their feet pounded the bare earth. The baying of the dog grew more distant and then more off to the side. For some reason, the dog had lost their scent—or had chosen to chase another one instead.

The breaking of branches in front of him caused him to stop short. He held a protective hand out toward Heather. A doe appeared through the trees. She stopped short when she saw Zane and Heather. Her tail flicked several times before she bounded off in a different direction.

Zane released a heavy breath. The sound of the dog had grown even dimmer. Maybe there was other wildlife around that had distracted the dog. They had only a precious few minutes to escape before the dog refocused and picked up their scent again.

Zane tried to picture the layout of the terrain in this area. Seven years was a long time. But some things didn't change. The river was still downhill. That much he knew, and it was still their best bet for getting out of here alive.

He turned a half circle and took off running. More crashing noises landed on his ears. More deer probably disturbed by the fire and the smoke it had created.

He spotted the silhouette of a man running from tree to tree. Zane stopped short and drew his gun out from his waistband. His gaze darted around. Where had the man disappeared to?

He detected movement behind one of the trees.

"Step out. I've got my sights on you," said Zane.

The man stepped out from behind the evergreen. Zane could barely make out any features beyond the covering of a beard and long hair.

The baying of the dog grew louder again. He'd found the trail again and was close.

The man held his hands up. "Go ahead. Shoot me."

Zane felt as though he'd been punched in the gut. The gun dropped to his side. He knew that voice.

Jordan, after all these years.

SEVEN

Heather watched in stunned silence as Jordan pulled his gun out and held it on Zane. She dared not run. Zane wasn't moving at all. He lowered his head and stared at the ground. Jordan's teeth curled back from his lip. The intensity in his eyes suggested he would pull the trigger if Zane gave him the slightest excuse.

What in the world was going on? Zane had blown their chance to get away.

The baying of the dog pressed on her ears. Other pursuers emerged through the trees.

"Restrain them," said Jordan.

Zane lifted his head at the sound of Jordan's voice. She thought she saw pain in his expression. The two men must have some kind of history. Clearly, Zane thought being captured was better than injuring Jordan so they could get away.

The other men drew close. Heather held out her hands to be restrained without putting up a fight. What was the use? They were outnumbered and outgunned. If they were going to escape, it would have to happen later—provided either she or Zane could come up with a plan.

Zane waited until the men stepped away from them. He leaned toward her and whispered. "I'll get us out of this."

"You could have gotten us out of this a minute ago." She spoke looking straight ahead, not wanting to draw their captors' attention. "Whose side are you on?" She snuck a glance at him.

Zane's face turned beet red and his jaw hardened.

Jordan waved his gun. "You two, stop talking."

They walked back through the woods in silence, both of them with their hands tied behind their backs. When they returned to the camp, the debris from the burned tents had already been gathered into a pile and stacked some distance from the undamaged tents.

Jordan indicated that Heather and Zane should be taken to the tent with the animal skins. Heather settled back where she'd sat previously.

Zane stared at the ground. "I meant it when I said I'd get us both out of here."

She shook her head, still stunned by his actions.

"I'm not one of them. You have to believe me," he said.

"But you used to be one of them. And clearly you still feel some loyalty to them, or at least to that animal, Jordan."

Zane continued to stare at the ground. "He's...he's not an animal." When he lifted his head his eyes were glazed. "He's my little brother."

The shock nearly knocked her over. Her throat went tight as guilt washed through her. "I am so sorry. I had no idea."

Zane shook his head as wrinkles formed on his forehead. "I got out. He didn't. I tried. I really tried to convince him not to stay with Willis." He looked off to the side as though some memory was playing through his mind.

A teenage boy stuck his head through the open flap of the tent. He set down a plate of food and a container of water before reaching inside and cutting the rope around Zane's hands. "Just you get to eat. Jordan says."

A chill ran down Heather's back. Of course they didn't need to feed her anymore. Her *usefulness* had expired.

As soon as the boy had left, Zane leaped across the tent and grabbed Heather's wrists to untie her. She felt a tug as he struggled to get the ropes loose.

"Wish they hadn't taken my knife," he said.

Jordan stuck his head in. "Always quick to act." He lifted the gun he held and aimed it at Heather. "And ready to rescue anyone who is in distress."

Heather cringed when the laser sight of the gun skittered across her chest. Jordan smirked at her fear before he let the gun fall to his side.

Jordan tilted his head toward the plate of food. "Eat up. Willis wants you in good spirits when he sees you."

Zane settled back down and took a bite of food.

"How many years has it been, little brother?"

Jordan jumped across the expanse of the tent and shoved the gun under Zane's chin. "Don't call me that."

Zane gently pushed his brother away and shook his head. "That is who you will always be to me." His voice was filled with compassion, which only seemed to make Jordan angrier.

"Shut up." Jordan shoved the gun in its holster, then moved across the tent and rolled up the sleeping bag.

The tent must belong to Jordan. He seemed to be preparing to not stay in it.

Heather eyed the gun. If her hands were free she was almost close enough to grab it. When she looked over at Zane, he was focused on Jordan's face and didn't seem to even notice the gun.

"You're looking a little ragged, Jordie. How long has it been since you've been to Fort Madison or anywhere civilized?" Zane's voice remained soft, without malice.

Jordan continued to pack up and avoid eye contact with his brother. "I know how to take care of myself." He spun around to face his older brother. "Only my friends call me Jordie."

"I didn't betray you. I don't know what lies Willis told you, but the truth is that I tried to find you for years."

Jordan continued to shove his belongings into a bag. Something in the jerky stop and start of his movements suggested Zane's words had an effect on him.

"Jordan, you're my little brother. We're blood." Zane's comment made Jordan twitch his head. Zane leaned closer to his brother. "Don't you remember after we got away from that home? I had your back and you had mine."

Jordan didn't respond. Instead, he became more frantic in his packing.

"We had some good times. Sleeping beneath the stars. Eating squirrel meat. You remember that?"

Jordan swung around and put his face very close to Zane's. "I know what you're trying to do."

"I'm not trying to trick you or get away." Zane tilted his head as his voice faltered. "I only want my brother back."

"Go ahead and try to grab my gun. I know you were thinking about it." Jordan's voice held a note of challenge.

"I wouldn't do that to you, Jordan. Not to my brother." Zane never broke off eye contact.

Watching the two men face-to-face was a study in contrasts. The younger was bitter, angry and wild. The older was filled with compassion and calm, showing love for his brother. Heather didn't know their whole story. What had happened to their biological parents that had cast them out into the world with just each other? She could not begin to imagine, but both of them had chosen different substitute fathers and it had made all the difference in the world.

Their gazes held for a long moment. Zane was not going to grab the gun even though he'd been given the opportunity. She only hoped his choice wouldn't cost them their lives.

Jordan broke off eye contact. "My brother died seven years ago."

Zane seemed to collapse in on himself. His shoulders slumped.

Jordan spoke without looking at his brother. "Eat the food and drink some water and don't think about escaping or untying her. I've got a guard posted outside." He flipped open the tent flap and crawled outside with his stuff.

The look of devastation on Zane's face was like an arrow through Heather's heart. She wanted to comfort him, but there was nothing she could say. She shook her head as her own eyes filled with tears.

"I had hoped that he wasn't too far gone." He lifted his head and looked at her. He scooted toward her and touched her cheek where a tear rolled down. "Thank you for caring." His eyes filled with warmth.

She felt a tug on her own heart as any doubt about Zane's true character washed away. He was a man of integrity and compassion.

"I never had a sibling. I can't begin to imagine…"

He lifted the container. "Do you want some water?"

She nodded.

He held the container to her lips and tilted it. The cool liquid felt good going down her parched throat.

He leaned toward her, placing the container on the ground. His lips brushed over hers, the moment of contact so fleeting that if the scent of his skin didn't linger in the air, she might have thought she'd imagined it.

Her heart pounded as affection reflected back through his eyes. "I meant what I said. I'll get us out of here."

She understood now that even though he was determined to get them both away from Willis and his men, the one thing Zane would not do was betray or harm his brother. For reasons she could not fathom, Zane still held out hope for Jordan. She prayed that hope would not get them killed.

Shouts of panic burst up from outside the tent, followed by gunfire. Footsteps pounded around the camp, mingled with the sounds of more upheaval and more yelling. Someone shouted something about a bear.

"Now is our chance," said Zane.

Zane grabbed Heather's wrists and tried to untie the knots of the rope that bound her. Jordan had taken all the knives and tools they could have used to cut her free. He searched the tent, coming up with a piece of metal. It would have to do. He sawed it across the ropes.

Outside, the gunfire grew farther away.

He finished freeing her. "Stay put." Using the tent flap as cover he peered outside, scanning the grounds for a moment before he ducked back in. "The guard isn't there anymore. He must have gone after the bear, too."

He slipped outside and stopped directly in front of the tent. The gunshots were spread apart and far away, and she thought she recognized the distinctive *zing* of a long-range rifle. Zane had given her a quick lesson about guns and rifles before they'd left Fort Madison.

Finally Zane moved away from the tent opening and signaled for her to come outside.

Her hand touched the dirt outside the tent as she crawled through. She lifted her head. No sign of Jordan or any of the other men. Zane tapped her shoulder and pointed toward a cluster of trees. Now she saw the plaid pattern of a flannel shirt nearly camouflaged by the evergreen boughs. Some men were still in the camp, still watching. The tracking dog remained in the middle of the camp, tied up and barking wildly. A boy emerged from the trees, untied the dog and pulled him back toward the cover of the forest, probably planning to use the dog to track the bear.

One of the men sprinted through the camp. Heather pressed closer to the tent, but the man didn't notice them. She didn't see Jordan anywhere.

Zane headed around the backside of the tent and she fell in behind him. There was no clear trail to follow. Zane seemed to know where he was going as he raced through the forest. The gunshots behind them died away.

They ran some distance until Zane stopped and

abruptly led them in a different direction. She had to trust that he knew where they were going. Her own navigation skills would only get them lost.

After they had sprinted for some time longer over rough terrain, Zane halted. He took a moment to catch his breath before he said anything. "There's an ATV around here. I covered it with pine boughs." He paced in one direction and then the other.

"Maybe we shouldn't waste time trying to find it," she said. Her gaze darted everywhere. She expected to see or hear Willis's men at any second.

"I can get you down to the river and across that other bridge much faster if we have it. It's a straight shot back to Fort Madison from there. Then I can come back up and try to extract Jordan."

Jordan clearly had no interest in leaving the group, but she understood why Zane wouldn't give up on his brother. So Zane's plan was to get her to safety and then put himself back in the line of fire, all for a little brother who has just stabbed him in the heart.

"I'll help you find it." For Zane, for the love he showed a brother, she would risk the loss of time in looking for the ATV.

Zane studied the silhouette of the mountain in the distance as though that would help him pinpoint the location of the vehicle.

"This way." He took off again running with intensity. She hurried behind him just as the distant baying of the dog landed on her eardrums. Now they were being tracked again. The past two days had already shown that these men were not going to give up easily. Willis must have some kind of sick psychological hold on them to make them so relentless and determined.

Heather pushed her legs to run faster. Her life depended on it. She did not see the unusual formation of pine boughs until they were only a few yards away from it. At a distance, no one would guess an ATV was hidden underneath.

Zane threw pine boughs to one side with a frantic strength and speed. She stepped in and helped uncover the one thing that gave them a chance against the men who were after them.

From time to time, the dog's persistent baying and barking erupted in the forest, a noise that made her chest tight.

Zane jumped on the ATV and started it. She got on behind him. He pushed the vehicle to its maximum speed as they bumped over the rough terrain. Twice they caught air. She held on tight, pressing her face against his shoulder.

Snow started to fall out of the sky again. Lazy, dizzy flakes twirling in the sky at first, but then the wind picked up and the snow seemed to come at them sideways. She huddled even closer to Zane, knowing that he was getting the brunt of the wind. They both were dressed for cold weather but she had lost her hat somewhere along the way. She pulled the hood of her jacket up over her head. Then she noticed Zane had no gloves. Steering the ATV in the cold and snow without them had to be miserable.

She tapped on his shoulder.

He brought the ATV to an idle. Snow stabbed her skin like a thousand tiny swords. She pulled her gloves off and draped them over his shoulder.

"They might be a little small."

He took the gloves and buttoned the top button on his coat. "Thanks. Pink is my color."

She managed to laugh, appreciating that he found humor despite the tension and fear hounding them.

Still, it didn't take long for apprehension to return while they sat there, unmoving. She shivered. The temperature had dropped at least ten degrees since they had taken off on the ATV.

Zane revved the engine, and she huddled in close to him, shielding her face as much as possible.

"Put your hands underneath my coat at my sides to keep them warm," he shouted over his shoulder.

The gesture, though practical, felt a little awkward to her. She slipped her hands beneath his coat, feeling his body heat as she rested them against the warm flannel of his shirt. Gradually, though, she felt herself relax. So much had changed since the previous night when he'd wrapped his arms around her at the fire to keep her warm. She knew Zane in a deeper way now. She saw him for who he really was—a good man trying to do the right thing.

Zane took off again. The terrain became even more treacherous as Zane angled the ATV downhill. She lifted her head to see over his shoulder. She couldn't see any sign of the river and wondered how far they still were.

The ATV slid sideways. Heather wrapped her arms tighter around Zane. He righted the vehicle but brought it to a stop shortly after coasting toward a cluster of trees.

"It's too slick." He craned his neck and spoke over his shoulder. "We need to wait this storm out."

She jumped off the back and stared down the mountain. Going on foot in the storm wouldn't be a good plan either.

Zane leaned close to look at the gauges on the ATV. "We have enough gas." Then he glanced up the mountain, a reminder that they were still being hunted even if they didn't see or hear their pursuers. He tapped the handlebars. "We can cover so much more ground with this." He tore off the gloves she'd given him and handed them back to her. "I only need them while I'm driving."

He grabbed a pine bough and placed it over the ATV. She gathered loose branches and helped him conceal the four-wheeler from view.

The wind and the cold had intensified even more by the time he grabbed her hand and led her to the shelter of some trees that formed a natural lean-to.

The overhang of branches made it seem darker as they huddled together for warmth.

She wanted to ask him how far it was to the river, but somehow she knew the answer would only make her feel more discouraged. Instead, she rested her head against his shoulder. The fatigue of having run so far on so little food and sleep, of having been so close to death overtook her. The tears slipped silently down her cheeks.

Doubt clouded her mind. Were they even going to get off this mountain and back to Fort Madison?

EIGHT

Zane stared out at the snow and listened to the wind whirling around and making the tree branches creak. Heather seemed to melt into his shoulder. He sensed that her mind had drifted a million miles from this cold fortress.

When she reached her hand up to swipe at a tear on her cheek, he knew she was falling apart. He couldn't blame her. He'd seen grown men break down and cry after days of being in the elements, and none of those men had had their lives threatened or had to flee like she had.

The one thing he didn't want was for her to give up hope. He knew his own strengths and capabilities and he was certain he would be able to take her across that river. And then he would get his brother away from Willis once and for all.

He'd seen Jordan start to soften even in the little bit of interaction they'd had. He had to believe he could get his brother back, mind, body and soul.

He returned his attention to Heather. He had to keep her spirits up or that would sink them faster than the cold or the men who were after them. "What are you thinking about?"

She took a moment to answer. "I was just thinking that if I was back in California right now, I would have just finished teaching my Pilates class. Then I might be getting ready to go for a swim or take my dog out for a run in the warm evening."

"Warmth. That sounds nice." He turned toward her. "Heather, I'm so sorry. I know this is way more than you bargained for. It's way more than *anyone* could have bargained for."

"I know you didn't intend for it to happen." She stared out at the falling snow. "It's just a lot to deal with. I don't see how we're going to get out of here."

"We'll make it." He wrapped his arm around her and squeezed her shoulder. He liked how she seemed to melt against him. When he'd kissed her earlier it had been impulsive. Not that he hadn't enjoyed it. But they were from different worlds. If they ever got back to those worlds, she would sell the business he loved and go back to the California sunshine she loved. She rested her head on his shoulder. Gradually, she relaxed even more. Her deep breathing told him that she'd fallen asleep. He kept watch and held still, not wanting to wake her.

The snow continued to fall as the sun sank lower in the sky. He had some tough choices to make. If he waited until nighttime, the headlights on the ATV would make them an easy target for anyone tracking them. If they hiked out on foot, they'd be fighting the storm and the clock.

The prudent thing to do would be to head out on the ATV before sunset. There was a risk of them wrecking in the adverse conditions and terrain, but it was a risk he was willing to take. The ATV would get them to safety so much faster.

He closed his own eyes, keeping an ear tuned to his surroundings. When he'd rested for what seemed like twenty minutes, he squeezed Heather's shoulder. "We need to get moving."

Her eyes popped open and fear penetrated her voice. "Did they find us?"

"No, we're fine. But we can't stay here any longer."

She nodded and jumped to her feet. Together they uncovered the ATV.

He fired up the machine and got on. She swung her leg over but then pointed at something over his shoulder. "What's that?"

He turned to look in the direction of her pointing. At first he couldn't see anything among the evergreens. He squinted. The snowfall made it hard to discern, but it looked like a plume of smoke rising up from the trees.

"Most likely a campfire," he said.

She leaned toward him so she could speak into his ear above the *parump parump* noise of the ATV engine. "Do you think it's them?"

Possible, but it could be hunters out scouting, too. Someone who would be in a position to help them. "We gotta find out," he said.

The ATV lurched forward and sped down the mountain. Twice they slid sideways. Heather held on and didn't even cry out. He glanced at the rising vapor of smoke. Hope stirred in his heart.

He stopped the ATV some distance from where the camp was. "I don't want them to hear us coming. Just in case." It didn't make sense for their pursuers to build a fire...unless they were setting another trap.

Heather dismounted. "Chances are it's not them, right? Why would they make camp? They're probably beating the bushes looking for us."

He cupped her shoulder. "Just what I was thinking. But let's not take any chances."

They moved with stealth through the trees as though they were a well-trained unit. Heather kept up with him, remained quiet and seemed to instinctually know when to push forward and when to remain put.

Zane lifted his head and sniffed at the scent of burning wood that hung in the air as they drew closer. He darted toward another tree.

He heard voices, a conversation on low volume. Two men, maybe. He pushed through the undergrowth to get a glimpse of them. The crackling fire was the first thing to come into view. Zane lowered a branch for a better view.

He'd been right—it was two men. They looked to be in their forties. He'd never seen either one of them before. Zane breathed a sigh of relief. These were not Willis's men. The men would have a brief exchange and then stare at the fire for a long time. Both of them wore hunter attire that looked brand new, not the tattered outerwear that characterized Willis's men. Two horses were tethered not too far from the fire.

Zane stepped into the clearing, holding up his hands in a surrender gesture. "Don't mean to bother you gentlemen. But we need your help getting back to Fort Madison."

He noticed that one of the men's eyes were round with fear. Of him? Did he look that threatening?

"I'm not here to hurt you. I'm a guide for Big Sky Outfitters."

"You ran into some difficulty, huh?" said the second man. His voice sounded stiff and unnatural.

Both men seemed nervous, much more so than he'd expect since they outnumbered him and were armed.

The men's guns were propped off to one side by a tree. Zane wondered if the men were poaching and feared getting caught.

"I don't want to make any trouble. I'm not the game warden." Zane held his palms toward the men in a surrender gesture. "We just need some help."

The first man kept angling his eyes off to the side but not moving his head. Zane felt the hairs on the back of his neck rise as he searched where the man seemed to be looking. He half expected to see a dead animal or a carcass. All he saw was bare ground.

"Who's *we* anyway?" said the second hunter.

Zane glanced over his shoulder. For some reason, Heather hadn't followed him into the clearing. Now he was on high alert. He took several steps back and saw a flash of movement in the trees.

This was an ambush, a trap. The second hunter looked directly at him and mouthed the word *run*.

A shot was fired and the hunter who had warned him slipped off the log he'd been sitting on and fell over, blood flowing from his shoulder. The first hunter dived toward where their guns were. But now there was only one gun there instead of two. Maybe Heather had taken the other one.

The hunters must have been told to act natural so Zane's guard would be down while Willis's men waited with their firearms trained on them for the right moment to capture him.

The second hunter didn't make it to his gun before he cried out in pain and gripped his stomach, scrambling toward the cover of the trees.

Zane dived for cover as the forest lit up like firecrackers from all the gunfire.

The gun battle stopped for a moment, and he heard an exchange of panicked whispering. He slipped farther into the trees.

To his side he heard voices, though he could not see anyone.

"Be careful, we don't want to kill him."

"Where did she go anyway? I don't see her anywhere."

Zane wondered that, too. Where *had* Heather gone?

Heart racing, Heather held on to the rifle she'd grabbed. Gunfire seemed to be coming from every direction. She backed away through the trees. A head popped up from behind a bush. She recognized him from the camp as one of Willis's men.

The man sneered at her as he stepped out toward her. His hand reached for his pistol.

She hit the man with the butt of the rifle, and he collapsed to the ground. She ran away from where the loudest gunfire was. By the time she stopped to catch her breath and rest her back against a tree, she was wheezing in air.

She'd never hit a man before in her life, but she couldn't bring herself to regret her actions. He would've taken her captive at gunpoint if she hadn't. Another volley of gunshots assaulted her ears. She cringed.

Hold it together, Heather. Think straight.

She stared up at the clouds drifting by while she held the rifle in her hand. It didn't look like the ones Zane had instructed her about before they left Fort Madison. Then she realized it wasn't a rifle at all. It was a shotgun. She'd seen one, even—once, long ago.

The gunfire died down. Had Willis's men succeeded in capturing Zane? There was only one way to find out.

Zane wouldn't leave her behind, so she knew she had to go back for him.

She circled back around toward the camp, pushing past her fear with each footstep.

She slowed as she drew near to the remnants of the fire. The air still smelled of wood smoke and cordite. The only noise she heard was the horses' frantic whinnying and the jangle of the metal on their bridles.

She dropped to the ground and worked her way to where she had a clear view of the camp. Her breath caught.

One of the hunters lay dead beside the smoldering fire.

Her stomach did a somersault and she tasted bile. She looked away. Finally, after several deep breaths, she steeled herself to take in the rest of the camp.

She detected no movement and heard nothing that sounded human. Rising to her feet, she ran through the center of the camp, past the dead man. A search of the edges of the area revealed that Zane and the others must have gone. All the tracks she could see led in the same direction. It didn't look like Zane had been able to escape. That had to mean that he was their captive again.

She ran back to where the horses were. Still clearly agitated, the horses jerked their heads up and down.

Her hands were shaking as she reached toward the first horse to untie him. She could cover a lot more ground with some transportation.

Once he was loose, the horse reared up. She stepped back, letting go of the reins. The animal galloped away, crashing through the forest.

Her heart was still racing from nearly having been trampled. She made soothing sounds as she stepped toward the second horse. She stroked the animal's neck and mane. She spotted a saddle not too far away. By the time she swung the saddle over his back and secured it around his belly, the animal had calmed down.

She shoved the shotgun into the leather holder attached to the saddle and untied her ride. She put her foot in the stirrup and got on, determined to find Zane—whatever it took, whatever it cost. They were in this together and they would get out of this together.

NINE

As he rushed away from the camp, Zane heard the frantic voices and movement but still didn't see anyone. Crawling commando style, he sneaked through the underbrush. He was pretty sure the hunter by the fire was dead. While the second one had rushed out of sight, Zane suspected he had been fatally injured, too. The hunters had probably planned to be up here for days or even a week. Family members would not be alarmed for some time. That meant there was no hope of the authorities showing up anytime soon.

He said a prayer for the dead men and their families.

The smart thing to do would be to try to make it back to the ATV and hope that Heather had the same plan.

He rushed from tree to tree, still hearing the occasional breaking twig. The snow had let up some but the cold still stung his face. When he got to where the ATV should have been, he saw that it had been stolen. There was a chance that Heather had gotten to it first, but he feared the worst. And the worst thing he could imagine was that Heather had been taken hostage again.

Maybe she'd been smart enough to grab a shotgun when the opportunity had presented itself. He'd spent some time showing her how a few different guns worked before they left town. A little instruction, though, was not the same as years of experience, and he hadn't told her anything about shotguns.

Several gunshots sounded behind him. His heart squeezed tight. He took off running toward where the gunfire had come from, slowing down and seeking cover as he drew close. He spotted a trail of fresh blood on the new-fallen snow. His heart squeezed tight. He wanted to call out Heather's name.

Instead, he backed up against the tree, listening and watching. No more disturbances. The men could be lying in wait, using Heather as bait once again. Or Heather could be hurt and bleeding.

He traced the blood trail with his eyes. His heart beat out an erratic rhythm. He heard more gunfire some distance from him and to the north. Maybe this was his chance. He had to know. Even if it was bad. Even if it showed him that he'd lost Heather just when she seemed to trust him.

He followed the blood trail into the quiet of the woods. He found the prone body of the second hunter. He checked for a pulse, but knew in his heart that he wouldn't find one. The man was dead, shot through the stomach and a second time through the arm. Zane closed his eyes and said a prayer.

He found the man's rifle a few feet from him. He still needed to locate Heather. He ran north toward where he'd heard the gunshots.

One of the horses that had been tied up at the hunters' camp galloped past him. Clearly agitated, the animal was kicking up snow and snorting, its hooves pounding the earth.

Once it was out of sight, Zane scanned the horizon and all the open areas, not seeing any movement. The silence bothered him. If he heard gunshots, it meant they were still after Heather, which meant she was still alive and running.

He jogged toward the last place he'd heard the gunshots, into the thick of the forest. He slowed, aware that a trap might have been set for him. A sense of helplessness descended on him like a shroud. He had to believe she was still alive. He wouldn't give up hope.

Maybe she was the one who had taken the ATV. He doubted she could navigate to the river crossing on her own, but she could at least get away fast.

Zane turned a half circle. A sudden stinging pain in his hand caused him to drop the rifle. Then his whole arm went numb. His stared down at his hand. It dripped with blood. He'd been shot. He felt lightheaded as he fought not to give in to the shock that pummeled his body.

He heard footsteps behind him and then voices.

"I told you it would work. I'm a good shot," said a young-sounding voice. "Willis just said bring him in alive." The voice sounded triumphant. "It's okay if he's hurt, don't you think?"

These were not men. They were boys barely in their teens. He swung around with the intent of knocking them to the ground with his good hand. No need to harm someone so young. All he needed to do was get away.

He lifted his arm to swing it, but the shock to his body from the wound slowed his movements. The boy he was aiming for had time to step back while his cohort dropped a hood over Zane's head. He swayed slightly from the blood loss.

"Come on, let's take him to Willis."

"Aren't we supposed to call in and wait for orders?"

"Casey took the radio, dude. Let's just take him up to Willis. We got him. We should get the credit."

As he listened to conversation, Zane could feel himself growing more and more light-headed. He needed to stop the bleeding in his hand before he passed out.

He heard the distinctive racking of a 12-gauge shotgun and then Heather's voice behind him, clear and strong. "I don't think anybody is going anywhere today, boys. Don't even think about reaching for your gun. Drop it on the ground right now, then take five steps back."

He heard a thud and footsteps.

"You've got ten seconds to disappear before I start shooting."

More footsteps. This time even more frantic.

Heather pulled the hood off Zane. He tried to focus on her beautiful face. Her gaze fell to his hand and the pool of blood on the ground. She pulled her scarf off and handed it to him. "Until we can get you a real bandage."

He wrapped the scarf around his bleeding hand. The bullet had gone through the fleshy area between his thumb and finger. "Where are the others?"

She tilted her head downhill. "I diverted them away from you and then circled back around to find you."

"Did you take the ATV?"

She shook her head. "I took one of the horses. Come

on, we've got to get out of this clearing." She grabbed his good arm above the elbow. "Are you going to be okay?"

He nodded but wasn't so sure it was the truth. He was having a hard time focusing and his stomach churned.

She grabbed the handgun the kid had surrendered and handed it to him. "It'll be easier to carry than that rifle."

She held on to him above the elbow and led him toward the trees. "We better hurry. I'm sure it's just a matter of time before they are able to tell the others our position."

"Those two don't have a radio, but I am sure they can find someone who does." Zane quickened his pace, though he still felt dizzy. "How did you know how to handle a 12 gauge? I never showed you."

Heather stuttered in her step. "I have a vague memory of my father showing me. It came back to me when I picked up the shotgun. I was too young to hold a gun but he explained things to me."

"Strange how memory works," he said.

Her gaze flashed toward him for just a moment. "Yes, I'm starting to wonder if it's why my father wanted me to come back here...so the memories would surface."

"If so, some of the memories might be ones you're better off without. I'm not sure Stephan was exercising sound judgment showing a five-year-old how to use a shotgun." He wondered what Stephan had been thinking, too, when the old man had written out his will. Though, in his defense, Stephan couldn't have foreseen the nightmare the two of them had been thrown into.

"Actually it was more of a safety lecture, and then he locked the gun back up," she said.

Heather glanced over her shoulder and then jogged toward a cluster of evergreens until the horse from the camp came into view. Heather untethered the horse from a branch.

She handed him the reins. "I don't know the way."

Zane mounted the horse struggling a little to do it one handed. He reached down his good hand for Heather.

She swung up behind him, wrapping her arms around him.

He led the horse out into the open and kicked the beast into a canter. He felt Heather's warmth as she held on and pressed close to him. The hand that had been shot was useless. He had to control the animal with only his good hand while he rested the other on his leg.

The light-headedness cleared, and he didn't feel like he might throw up anymore.

The trail before him was easy enough to navigate. He leaned closer to the horse's neck and spurred the animal to go faster. Heather leaned forward as well. They seemed to be functioning as a single unit, each of them knowing what to do without saying anything.

The horse kicked up snow and dirt as it traversed the flatter part of the landscape. The animal slowed once the trail became more winding. Horses weren't as sure-footed as mules, but on this kind of terrain, it was better transport than an ATV.

Zane's mind turned to the horse's owners—the hunters who now lay dead in the forest. They'd been up in the high country without a guide, so they must be local men. Zane might have even seen them before, at the grocery store or the post office. And now they were gone. The damage Willis could do was astounding. Zane vowed that when he got down off this mountain, he'd find the hunters' families and speak to them himself. It was the least he could do.

Willis was usually careful to keep a low profile. Killing was unlike him. And now with three dead men to account for, Willis must be planning something big for him to risk the consequences of being found out. But what could he possibly be after that could be that important? And what did any of it have to do with Zane?

He stared down the series of switchbacks on the trail. A fire had burned out most of the trees on this part of the mountain, providing him with a clear view of much of the trail.

Men were moving up the trail far enough away that they looked like bugs. All of them were dressed in camouflage or earth tones. Most likely Willis's men had gotten the message and were headed back up the trail.

Zane brought the horse to a halt. "Dismount. We need to find a different way down this part of the mountain to get to the river."

Zane swung off the horse and hurried into the thick of the forest with Heather at his heels.

The men were moving at a rapid pace up the mountain, six of them in all. At best, they had a five-minute head start over their pursuers. Not good.

TEN

Even as they sprinted through the trees, Heather felt a heaviness descend. Were they ever going to get out of these mountains? "Is there another way to get to the river?" she asked between deep breaths. Zane quickened his pace and she struggled to follow. "They're watching our access points to it too closely."

"I've been thinking the same thing," Zane agreed. "There *is* another way to get out of here. We won't end up in Fort Madison, though. We'll have a long hike after that to get to civilization."

He stopped and dropped the reins. "We're going to have to let the horse go. It's not a route he can traverse."

Her spirits sank even lower. The horse had seemed like an answer to prayer. "What about the 12 gauge?"

"Carry it if you want, but I think it will slow you down."

After thinking for a moment, Zane mustered up a half smile for her and said, "The horse might work as a diversion." Zane coaxed the horse until it was turned around and then slapped its flank. The animal took off running, making a beeline for the trail. Zane took her gloved hand. "This way."

Her calves strained as they climbed a steep incline away from the trail. Down below, the shouts of the men filled the forest. They must have spotted the horse.

Their voices struck a note of fear inside of her. They were outnumbered and outgunned. Were they ever going to get away or would they be hunted to the point where exhaustion and hunger forced them to surrender?

As though he sensed her losing hope, he squeezed her hand. "Let's put some distance between us and them then we can rest."

The noise of the pursuers faded when they worked their way through the thick trees. They walked for what seemed like hours before Zane let go of her hand. "I think we lost them. We can build a small fire. Find an area where the trees and brush provide a degree of cover." He reached inside his jacket. "There's the fire-starter kit. I'm going to go find something for us to eat."

She took the pouch and headed toward the thicker part of the forest. Zane pulled the pistol out of his waistband and disappeared into the grove of trees. She worried that they weren't far enough away and that a gunshot would alert the men to their position, but she reminded herself that Zane knew what he was doing. She needed to do her part and not question his choices.

She walked a short distance until she found a small open area in the thick of the trees. She couldn't see anything through the brush, so she kept her ears tuned to the sounds around her while she knelt after gathering twigs and several logs.

She opened Zane's waterproof container, which held the fire starter. She felt paper beneath the container.

Zane had inadvertently given her two photographs that he must always keep in his inside pocket. One was of a much younger Zane with another boy who was maybe twelve years old. They were sitting in front of a Christmas tree. She stared at the photo for a long moment before she figured out the younger boy must be Jordan.

She examined the second photograph, Zane with an older man. The older man had his arm around Zane as they stood outside by an evergreen, both of them holding rifles. She had never seen a picture of her father and her memories of him were still vague, blurry. But the resemblance was impossible to ignore. The eyes that looked back at her were her eyes. The photos were undamaged from when they'd fallen in the river.

A faint gunshot somewhere in the distance brought her back to the present moment. She stuffed the photos into the waterproof container and set to building a fire. She dug through the pouch for the dryer lint. Flames consumed the lint and then the twigs. She placed her hands close to the heat and then gathered some sticks that were close by.

She heard a rustling in the trees and looked up to see Zane holding a dead rabbit. "Dinner."

Her stomach growled. She would have turned her nose up at wild rabbit in the past, but now she would eat anything and be grateful.

Zane skinned the animal with a pocketknife he must have snatched from somewhere since his bigger knife had been taken.

Finding the two photographs helped her see him in a different light. They were pictures of the two people who meant the most to him. It was very telling that he seemed to carry them with him everywhere he went.

"Something on your mind?" Zane caught her staring.

"No, nothing." She looked away as heat rose up on her cheeks. She remembered what Zane said about not letting the fire get too big and only placed another log on in when it threatened to die down.

She glanced back up at him. A faint smile graced his face. When she had first met him, she'd thought he was some kind of wild man with his long hair and beard. She had only assumed that her father was the same way if they got along so well. Zane was way more complicated than that. Did that mean that her father had been too?

"I was just thinking about my...my dad."

He stuck the rabbit on a sharp stick he'd fashioned and placed it close to the fire. "Your dad?"

It felt strange to even call him that. "Tell me something about him that would surprise me."

Zane rotated the stick. "He liked poetry."

"Poetry?"

"Not moon, spoon, June stuff either. Sometimes in the evening he'd read out loud around the fire while we settled down. He always started off with a psalm. They were his favorite, but he liked Robert Frost, too."

She'd read Robert Frost as a teenager. "That does surprise me." But it was a good surprise. Well, mostly good. The news made her feel closer to the father she barely remembered but sad at the same time for all that she had missed. "My mother said he used to steal the grocery money so he could spend it on liquor."

"That is not the man I knew. I wish you could believe that."

"It's just hard to let go of all the ugly things my

mother said about him, the stories she told that made me hate him."

She didn't think her mother had been lying. Stephan had been a drinker. It had probably been the smart, safe choice for them to leave him. But after they'd gone... was there a chance he really had changed? She was starting to believe that maybe such a transformation was possible. If Zane could have changed so dramatically just by being under Stephan's influence, maybe her father could have changed, too. Jordan represented what Zane would have become if he hadn't gotten away from Willis.

Confusion whirled through her like a hurricane. She hadn't had much time to think about her father since Willis's men had come after them.

Zane lifted the now blackened rabbit from the fire. "I think this is about ready to serve." He laid it on a flat stone he'd brought with him. "My hand still isn't working real well. Would you carve?" He handed her the pocketknife. "I'll hold it in place."

She flicked open the knife and cut into the meat. She drew her hand back when she touched the smoldering flesh.

"Careful, it's kind of hot," Zane said.

"I got that. That's what fire does. I just wasn't thinking." Her own stupidity made her shake her head. She offered Zane a quick glance. Amusement danced in his eyes, too.

"We all have our space cadet moments," he said.

The sparkle in his eyes. The warmth of his voice. The way she felt close to him. She could get used to those things about Zane.

She cut off a chunk of meat. The two of them ate

in silence. She hadn't realized how hungry she was until the first bite of food made her mouth water and her empty stomach cry out. The meat was stringy and charred but it was better than any lobster she had had off the pier.

After they both had eaten all the meat she'd cut away, Zane pointed to the carcass. "There's still meat on the bones if you want more."

She patted her stomach. "I think I'm full." She warmed her hands over the tiny fire.

Zane finished the rest of the meat and tossed the bones. He stared at the sky. "We better get going."

They put out the fire and stepped out into the open. The sun was low in the sky as they headed up the steep incline.

How long would it be before Willis and his men figured they'd given up on getting out by way of the river?

"How many men and boys are with Willis?" Heather asked.

"The number is hard to figure out. When I was with him, there were a number of people who lived in town who helped him and sympathized with his crazy beliefs, and then there were the true believers who stayed with him in the wild."

"How many of those were there?"

Zane stopped walking, tilted his head toward the sky, probably to mentally count. "Maybe thirty men and boys back then. I doubt the number has changed much. He always finds his share of new boys, but not everyone sticks around. Some—like me—leave by choice. Others get arrested for a variety of crimes, or recognized as runaways and brought to the authorities."

Her chest squeezed tight. They'd seen at least twenty

men and boys. "Are they scattered all over the high country?"

"Willis liked to have several camps. He figured that made us stronger. If the law came down on one camp, he wouldn't lose all his men at once." He walked for several more steps. "I doubt he has changed his strategy."

They pushed on through the night until darkness descended, slowing their progress.

Zane pressed close to Heather. "I know it's hard to see, but I think we should keep going."

She picked up on the urgency in his voice. "Did Willis always camp in the same place?"

"He moved around, but he had some favorite hideouts."

She wondered if they were close to one of those hideouts but was afraid to ask. Her heart was already beating fast enough and every cell in her body was on high alert. If she had learned anything in the last two days of running, it was that she should never let her guard down.

They walked in silence with the stars twinkling above them. Her own breathing and the pounding of their footsteps created a strange harmony. They separated slightly, but she could still tell where he was by the sound of his boots padding across the hard earth.

Her foot gave way beneath her. She stumbled then fell, rolling several feet. Darkness surrounded her.

"Zane?" Her heartbeat drummed past her ears. Every second he didn't answer, panic embedded deeper into her. "Zane?"

Clouds rolled by above her and she reached out to climb up the incline she'd tumbled down.

She heard a voice above her.

"There you are," Zane said. The voice drifted down to her, though she couldn't even make out his silhouette.

She let out a heavy breath. His voice was a comfort in the darkness.

"It's just so dark. I lost you in an instant," he said. "Are you hurt?"

"I don't think so. I didn't fall that far." She was beginning to wonder how prudent it was to travel by night without any light. "If you could give me your hand?"

No response.

"Zane?"

She scrambled up the rocky incline, feeling for solid ground. Instinct told her not to cry out again. She'd probably given away their position by crying out in the first place.

Instead, she crouched and listened. It took a few minutes for her to parse through the sounds that were just a part of the forest to hear something that might have been a grunt and one man punching another.

She crawled closer, waiting and listening, while her heart pummeled her rib cage.

This time the sound of flesh hitting flesh was more distinct. Still on all fours, she made her way toward the sound. Her knee jammed against some rocks, causing several to roll. She froze, fearing the noise had given her away.

Light flashed in her peripheral vision. Before she could turn toward the light source, clawlike hands dug into her shoulders, flipped her around and landed a blow to her jaw. Pain radiated through her whole face and down her neck. Her eyes watered.

She rolled onto her belly and struggled to get to her feet. In the darkness, hands grabbed at the hem of her coat. She thrashed, seeking to get away from her invisible assailant even as he grabbed her arm. She punched the air, hoping to hit something. Finally her hand connected with flesh. A voice grunted in protest and the grip on her arm loosened.

She turned and ran, stumbling over the rocks and veering away from where she'd fallen. Getting an idea, she slowed her steps. Maybe she could cause her pursuer to fall in the same way she had.

She kicked some rocks, making noise on purpose. Light flashed again. She saw the silhouette of a man just as he took a step toward her.

Her heart pounded. Adrenaline coursed through her body. She planted her feet, waiting, listening to the rapidly approaching footsteps. When it sounded like the man was close enough to grab her, she slid to one side as quietly as possible.

Rocks crashed against each other. The man screamed. She moved to get away from the incline, but she'd waited too long. A hand reached up and grabbed her ankle, pulling her down. She twisted around and landed on her butt. The impact sent vibrations of pain up her spine.

She kicked with the leg that was still free but only connected with air. The man pulled her down even more. She flipped over on her stomach, clawing at the rocky surface to get leverage.

A light blazed off to the side. This time it remained on and another man approached her. His foot pressed on her hand.

She wasn't about to cry out in pain.

"Let's quit this dog and pony show." The voice

was Jordan's. He shouted down at the other assailant. "Get up. We've wasted too much time." Jordan pulled Heather to her feet and yanked her hands behind her.

The venom she heard in his voice sent shivers down her back.

Jordan shouted at the man who had fallen down the incline. "Crawl up out of there and let's get moving." Jordan pressed Heather's hands together and wrapped rope around them.

He pushed on Heather's back. "March, double time."

He switched on his flashlight and used it to point. "That way." He held his gun up so she could see it. "Trot and don't try anything."

As she took a step, Heather tried to calm herself with a deep breath. Was he marching her into the woods to shoot her or was she still *useful*?

"Did you catch Zane, too?" She purged her voice of the fear that had invaded every cell of her body. Was this the end for her?

Jordan didn't say anything.

Heather stopped and turned sideways.

He lifted his gun. "Keep going. Toward those trees."

His voice gave nothing away.

If this was the end for her, she had to let Jordan know how much Zane cared about his brother. "He keeps a picture of you two together when you were kids."

Jordan's hand clamped on her shoulder, and he spun her around. His face was close enough to hers that she could see the whites of his eyes even though he held the flashlight at an angle. "I know what you are trying to do. You're lying to me so you can try to break me."

She held his gaze despite the terror that raged

through her for her own life. "No, Jordan, that's not what I am trying to do. I'm telling you the truth."

An emotion flickered across his face, and then the curtains seemed to come down over his eyes again, giving them that glazed look of the brainwashed. "My brother left me."

"He left *Willis*, not you."

That little moment of vulnerability she'd witnessed gave her hope. Maybe she wouldn't live to see it, but Zane might get his brother back.

Jordan's features hardened. Whatever door had been opened had slammed shut. "Turn around and march toward those trees. I can't believe how much time we've wasted."

That was the second mention of wasted time. Whatever it was they had planned, it must have become more urgent.

Heather made her way toward the trees wondering if she had only minutes to live.

ELEVEN

Zane's head hurt where he'd been hit with the butt of a gun and his hand ached from the gunshot wound. He'd fought hard against the three other men who ambushed him. But in the end, he'd lost. One of the men continued to hold a gun on Zane, even though Zane's hands were bound.

Zane had no idea what had happened to Heather. They'd gotten separated in the fight and darkness.

The second man watched from a distance, a sneer on his face. All of the men were older, better equipped and better trained than the teenagers and young men he and Heather had first encountered.

Static sounded on the second man's radio. He pressed a button and turned away, talking in low tones. All Zane could pick up on was a lot of "yes sir, no sir" remarks.

When he got off the radio, he signaled for the third man who Zane recognized as John, the man he'd stolen the ATV from. They put their heads together, and then the John picked something off the ground and stalked toward Zane. Once he was close enough, Zane could see that the man held a hood.

He wasn't leaving without a fight. Zane put his head down and charged toward John, who held the hood, knocking him down. The man with the gun grabbed him from behind and hit him once again in the head. Zane buckled to his knees as black dots filled his vision.

The man with the gun leaned over and picked up the hood, placing it over Zane's throbbing head.

"You just never quit fighting, do you?" said the man with the gun. "You don't need to see where you're going, pal."

He was led some distance through the trees. He had no idea where they were headed other than they were pointed north. The wind gusted around him. He felt a tap on his shoulder.

"Get on the ATV," said John.

Zane estimated that they traveled over steadily rising terrain for at least twenty minutes before they stopped, and his captors commanded him to dismount. He was led along another path. He smelled a dampness that indicated they were near a cave.

A hand was placed on top of his head, and he ducked down. He was commanded to sit, and he obeyed. Fading footsteps indicated someone had left the area, but he sensed that someone else was still in the cave with him.

The warmth from a fire covered his face and chest. He sat on a thick animal fur. He heard the grunting of someone repositioning himself. The fire crackled.

Zane had a pretty good idea who was in the room with him. Willis liked to play psychological games. The silence was meant to intimidate him. As a young man, he might have fallen victim to the games and tricks Willis used, but no more. He could wait out the master manipulator if need be.

With the hood still on his head, Zane closed his eyes and prayed. More than anything, he hoped that Heather was okay.

Willis was the first to break the silence. "Been a long time, Zane."

Zane did not respond. He just kept praying.

"Pull his hood off," Willis barked.

A hand grabbed the hood and yanked. The guard stepped back and pressed against the cave wall, still holding the hood. It took a moment for Zane's eyes to adjust to the dim light. He spotted another guard at the entrance of the cave.

His eyes traveled around, assessing the possibility for escape. He let his eyes wander for a long time, knowing the man wouldn't appreciate being ignored. If he could get the man to lose his temper, he might slip and release some information that Zane could use. But finally his eyes turned to his old mentor.

Willis had white hair in a buzz cut. His clean-shaven face revealed high cheekbones. Though his skin was leathery from time spent outdoors, his slim physique made him appear much younger than his fifty or so years. As always, he was in top athletic shape.

Willis lifted his chin. "Heard the old man died." His voice took on a mocking tone. "Too bad."

The remark was meant to sting, to put Zane on the defensive about the man who had meant so much to him. Though his heart ached at the mention of Stephan's death, Zane gave nothing away in his expression.

"I suppose you're wondering what all this cat-and-mouse stuff has been about." Willis flicked away debris on his shirtsleeve.

"You never play a game just to play a game."

"True." Willis rose to his feet and stared down at Zane. Nothing Willis did was an accident. The change in position was meant to dominate Zane. "It seems we need your expertise."

Zane was sure the expertise referenced was not his ability as an outfitter. Willis knew this mountain better than anyone.

"The man who trained you to build thermite bombs has to serve a lengthy prison sentence," Willis said.

A bomb. One of Willis's plans had always been robbing banks using explosives—usually on commission to acquire an item someone wanted. An enemy to any authority other than his own, Willis enjoyed making the bank employees and customers feel threatened and exposed by breaking down the security they took for granted, and the money he made from acquiring the item for his own customer helped keep his ragtag group in supplies.

Zane had been in training to help with that goal when he left the group. Thermite bombs were designed to melt metal at high temperatures. Willis must have either been hired or gotten wind of a low-security bank that had something of value in it. A thermite bomb would melt a vault door. "You know I won't build something that destructive."

The robberies took place after-hours, and the instructions were always to disable any security guards rather than kill—Willis knew better than to provoke the kind of manhunt that killing indiscriminately would cause—but there was still a chance of people getting seriously hurt. It had happened before.

Willis shook his head. "How did I know that would be your response?" He lifted his chin toward the guard by the door, who immediately left the cave.

A moment later, the guard returned with Heather in tow. Zane's chest went tight. She had a gag in her mouth, and her eyes held a haunted quality. Rage rose up inside of him. If they had hurt her...

Willis continued to talk as though he didn't even see Heather. "Now we have gone to some trouble to gather all the materials for you, and you *will* comply."

Willis didn't have to say "or else" to get his message across. If Zane didn't build the bomb, Heather would die and probably be tortured first.

"What did you do to her?"

"Relax. We just made her run a little. You know hurting women is not my thing." Willis's tone remained casual, as though they were two men exchanging fishing stories.

Willis lifted his chin toward the guard, who picked Heather up and dragged her to the cave entrance. The look of fear in Heather's eyes as she gave Zane a backward glance cut him to the bone.

Willis leaned close to Zane's ear. "I trust you'll want to get started right away."

Zane resisted the urge to hurt Willis. Rage coursed through him like hot lava, but he kept his expression neutral as Willis straightened.

"Take him to where he needs to be." Willis turned his back.

The second guard sprang into action. Resolve formed inside Zane. He wasn't going to build the bomb, but he had to find a way to escape and get Heather free, too.

As they walked out of the cave and through forested areas, Zane could pick out several camouflaged tents. Was Heather in one of those? He had to find out where they were keeping her.

Whatever it took, he was going to get Heather and himself out of this compound. And he would do everything in his power to prevent the attack Willis had planned.

The guard pulled Heather through the brush until he came to a hole similar to the one she'd fallen into days ago.

"I'll undo your hands. You lower yourself down by that rope." The young man pointed toward a mud-soaked climber's rope.

A weariness had set into Heather's bones. Though the guard looked to be barely out of his teens, she knew trying to escape would be an act of futility. If he didn't catch her, one of the other men she saw wandering around would. Her hands gripped the rope, and she slid down to the bottom of the pit. A layer of straw covered the mud floor. The guard threw a dirty backpack down to her, pulled up the rope and covered the hole with a lid woven from sticks and tree boughs. A little moonlight filtered through the tiny holes.

Heather collapsed on the straw and opened the backpack, which contained a canteen, jerky and dried fruit. She ate the fruit and had a sip of water. She rose and wandered around the deep pit. It was a good twenty feet to the top, and there was no place on the slick muddy walls to get a grip. She took her boot off and used it as a trowel to try to dig a foothold in the wall. Her hands became muddy from the effort, but eventually she made some progress. She stood back to catch her breath.

By the time she had started on the second foothold, the sky had grown darker. Voices and footsteps alerted her to someone approaching. She dived back down on the straw, slipping her foot without the boot under her leg and hiding the boot under the backpack. The lid to the hole was drawn back. She shielded her eyes as a flashlight beam shone in her face. Her heartbeat kicked into high gear. If they saw the holes, she'd be dead.

The man shining the light on her appeared in silhouette. Finally he pulled back, taking the light off her and then placing the cover on the hole again. How many times in the night would they check on her? She waited until she heard fading footsteps before jumping up. She felt along the wall to where she'd been digging. After some time, she was muddy and out of breath, but the second foothold was in place.

Loud rock music played in the distance. She heard voices shouting and guns being shot.

She shoved her foot that still had a boot on it in the first foothold and placed her hand in the second hole in order to dig the third one. Her bare foot grew cold as she reached up and dug into the muddy wall. The task would take forever. She had to keep jumping down to rest from the strain on her muscles.

Approaching footsteps made her resume her position on the ground by the backpack. The lid slid back and a rope came down.

"Climb up. We need you," a disembodied voice said.

She hurried to put her boot on. "Can you give me a

second? I was sleeping." She wiped her muddy hands on the backpack, rose to her feet and gripped the rope. "Okay, I'm ready." She tried to climb, but her arms felt weak. "Can you help me a little?"

Even her body had its limits. Two days of running with little food and sleep was taking a toll.

She felt a tug on the rope as she held on and was pulled up. She reached out for solid ground, climbed to the surface and let go of the rope. A hand gripped the back of her shirt and lifted her up.

Off in the distance, a huge fire had been built. Men danced around, shooting guns and playing loud music. She saw the glow of lanterns in several tents.

The man behind her pushed on her upper back. "Get moving."

They walked away from the camp into the darkness of the forest. Her heart seized up. Was this man going to shoot her?

She slowed down. He punched her shoulder blade.

"Where are we going?"

He didn't answer.

Her chest squeezed even tighter.

She took several more steps deeper into the forest.

"Stop here." His voice was devoid of emotion.

Heather swallowed to try to produce some moisture in her mouth. She couldn't get a deep breath.

"Put your hands behind your back." He poked her with the hard barrel of a gun.

She did as he said and the man wrapped rope around her hands and jerked it tight.

"Don't try anything." The man stepped out in front of her, got down on all fours and proceeded to pat the ground.

Her heart raged against her rib cage. It felt like her chest had been wrapped with a tight bandage. What was going on here?

The man swung open a door on the forest floor. Light flooded out.

He turned to face her. "Go down those stairs."

She took a step toward what looked like some kind of underground bunker. She placed her foot on the first wooden step.

"Don't even think about running. I have a gun pointed at you," said the man.

She stepped down the remainder of the stairs. The door above her closed. Glancing around, she saw that the bunker had concrete walls lined with stacks of food, cots and a machine that was probably a generator. A guard stood in a corner. Zane sat at a table, pieces of metal, wire and containers in front of him. The hand that had been shot was wrapped in a fresh bandage.

A look of shock filled Zane's features when he saw her.

She must be a muddy mess. "I'm okay. They didn't hurt me."

The guard stalked toward her. "Shut up." He grabbed her shirt at the shoulder and dragged her toward a chair.

"Don't treat her that way." Zane lurched toward her, but was stopped by the chain around his foot.

The guard pushed her down into the chair and then took his position back against the wall.

She raised her head to meet Zane's gaze.

"No talking," said the guard as his hand brushed over the gun holstered on his waist.

Zane raised his eyebrows and attempted a smile as if to lift her spirits. The gesture in such dire circumstances warmed her heart. She lifted her chin, trying to give him a positive message back.

Between them was a large wooden box holding a revolver. The guard remained in the corner, his hand hovering over his own gun.

The only sound in the room was a clock ticking away the seconds.

Zane stared at her, and she kept her gaze on Zane. She saw compassion in his eyes. The clock kept ticking. The room felt unusually warm. Sweat poured past her temples. She fixated on the gun in the box.

Clearly someone was playing some sort of sick psychological game. She pulled her gaze away from the gun and stared at Zane. Looking into his eyes was the only thing that made her feel safe.

A door scraped open to the side of her. She turned her head. No one stepped out. Minutes passed. More game playing. Trying to increase her fear.

She turned again to look at Zane. He shook his head and shrugged his shoulders, a gesture that was meant to reassure her, but she saw the fear behind his eyes.

She heard footsteps and the door opened farther. Finally, the lean older man with a short buzz cut she'd seen earlier in the cave stepped into the concrete room. He crossed his arms over his muscular chest. His smile sent chills down Heather's spine. His eyes were an icy blue. When she had first seen him, the arrogance and the air of authority he gave off told her the man must be Willis.

He signaled to the guard, who walked across the room, picked up the revolver and spun the cylinder around before locking it in place. He put the gun back down on the table.

"It seems Mr. Scofield here thinks it's okay to try to trick me." Willis shifted his weight and crossed his arms over his chest. "By hiding some of the chemicals needed to make this bomb work." Willis took a few steps toward Zane, combat boots pounding on the concrete. "There is always a price to pay for betrayal."

A long moment of tense silence was followed by the tapping of footsteps. Someone else was coming into the room. The door creaked open even wider and Jordan entered.

He stepped toward Heather. Her whole body stiffened. She glanced at Zane, who had gone completely white.

Jordan looked over at Willis, who gave him a nod. Then Jordan picked up the gun on the table and pressed it against her temple. The room seemed to be spinning. She tried to focus on Zane. Her vision blurred. She couldn't tell what he was trying to communicate with his expression. Her breath caught in her throat.

Jordan pulled the hammer back and placed his finger against the trigger. She squeezed her eyes shut and the trigger clicked.

Nothing happened.

Her whole body was shaking as her eyes blinked back open.

Jordan pulled the gun away from her head, turning slightly toward Willis.

Heather glanced toward Willis, who nodded. "Again," he said.

"No, please." She looked over at Zane, expecting to see rage for what was happening to her. Instead, he offered her a small shake of her head. He was trying to tell her something. How could she feel reassurance with a gun pointed toward her head?

Jordan placed the gun on her temple again. She gulped in air as tears streamed down her face. Was she going to die here? She lifted her head, locking onto Zane's gaze. Now she saw the warmth and compassion she'd searched for. His eyes seemed to be almost pleading with her.

It must be tearing him up to know that his brother was this brainwashed.

Again Jordan pulled the hammer back. A long moment passed before he placed his finger against the trigger.

Heather bit her lower lip and held her breath. The trigger clicked. She cringed, expecting a blast and then darkness.

She opened her eyes to the concrete room and took in a sharp breath. Zane was still there staring at her, trying to communicate something with his eyes.

It felt as though an elephant was sitting on her chest.

Willis's voice pelted her. "That's probably enough for now. I'm sure Mr. Scofield finally sees the error of his ways."

The guard lifted Heather off the chair. Her knees buckled, and she struggled to stand up. Her legs were as limp as cooked noodles.

The guard half dragged, half carried her to the door. He knocked on the door with his gun. The door swung open, metal hinges creaking. Another guard peered down.

"Take her back." The guard pushed Heather toward the stairs. It took all her strength to walk up them.

The second guard grabbed her shoulder and pulled her up. She took a few steps and fell on the ground.

Her knees pressed into the snowy earth. She was still shaking from the emotional torture she'd endured.

"Get up."

She stared at the ground. "Please give me just a moment." She tried to get to her feet but collapsed.

"Fine, I'll take you to medical." The guard lifted her up and roughly carried her to a tent. He dropped her on the tent floor. "Get in there and wait."

With her hands still tied behind her back, she scooted inside the tent. Through the open tent door, she could see the guard pacing outside.

The revelry by the fire had died down, though she still heard occasional shouts and gunfire. Willis's army was finally settling down for the night.

A man poked his head inside the tent. He studied Heather for a moment and then crawled inside. He carried a backpack with him that had a red cross on it.

"Anything broken?"

She shook her head.

He unzipped a pocket on the backpack and pulled a flashlight out. "I need to check your eyes."

She recoiled.

"I'm not here to hurt you in any way. That is somebody else's job."

He turned the light up on the lantern that sat in the middle of the tent. Heather thought she detected a hint of compassion in his voice. Something she had witnessed in none of Willis's other followers.

"Are you a doctor?"

"Combat medic. Iraq. Three tours."

He shone the light in both her eyes. The man seemed almost normal. "Why are you here with Willis?" she asked.

"I have PTSD that led to episodes of violence. I don't fit into polite society anymore. When everyone I knew turned their back on me, Willis took me in."

"My name is Heather."

He stopped rummaging through his bag and met her gaze. "I'm Nathan. You look pretty shook up. Do you want a sedative?"

The last thing she needed was to be sedated. "No."

"Then I'll just recommend that you be sent back to wherever they're keeping you."

She leaned toward him, wishing she could make a connection with him by touching his arm, but her hands were bound behind her. "Please, I need your help."

He pulled away. "Forget it, lady. I never want to get on the wrong side of Willis. The guy gives me three squares a day, and all I have to do is stitch men up when they bleed." His raised his voice as though he wanted whoever was listening outside to hear. Then he leaned closer to Heather. "I'm bugging out. Willis is planning on robbing the bank in Fort Madison. He got word that some rich guy just put a bunch of valuables in the safety deposit boxes. The other guys are acting like it's totally normal, just another day on the job. I didn't know they were like that when I joined up. I can't be a party to the things they're willing to do."

"Can you go down and warn the bank?"

"I've got my own legal troubles that keep me out of town. I'll take my chances living on my own in the wilderness."

Before she could react, Nathan moved toward the door of the tent and shouted, "She's ready to go."

He dug into his pocket and threw an object by her hands before leaving the tent.

She scooted on her bottom a little to grab the object. Her hand wrapped around cold metal. Nathan had thrown her a pocketknife. A guard stuck his head into the tent. She gripped the knife in her fist to hide it.

"Let's get moving," said the guard.

She worked her way toward the tent door while he stood outside waiting. Strength had returned to her legs. She gripped the pocketknife, hoping the guard wouldn't notice. He pushed her in a different direction than the pit she'd been left in before.

The guard pointed toward a small shed. "Nathan thought you would do a little better aboveground." He opened the door.

She stepped inside the dark space and slipped down to the floor. She was exhausted, and the trauma of having a gun to her head had taken its toll on her body, but she needed to find a way to escape and to get Zane free, as well.

She flipped the knife around in her hand until she could open it and saw away at the rope that bound her. As she worked, she tried to come up with a plan. She had a better feel for the layout of the camp. The place where they were keeping Zane was away from everything else. That might help in being able to secure his freedom unnoticed.

Time was of the essence. The cover of darkness was one of the only things working in her favor right now. She sawed on the rope and prayed that she and Zane could get out of here alive.

TWELVE

"You get an hour to sleep." Jordan didn't make eye contact when he approached where Zane was working.

Zane couldn't bring himself to look at his brother either. Was Jordan so far gone that he was indifferent to the cruel torture he'd put Heather through?

Zane knew Willis's games, and he'd seen that the gun didn't have even one bullet in it. Willis needed Heather alive for now to use as leverage until the bomb was complete. The stunt had been to scare her, not to actually hurt her. He had tried to communicate that to her without much success.

Jordan tossed a key on the table so Zane could undo his shackles. Zane knelt down and stuck the key in the slot. He knew without looking that Jordan had a gun trained on him. The betrayal hurt.

This was his little brother. They'd stood holding hands at their parents' funeral, shivered together in the dark and cold when they'd run away from foster care, protected and taken care of each other. But now his brother had become someone he didn't know at all.

Zane placed the key on the table and Jordan leaned to get it.

He couldn't give up. Jordan was blood. As repulsed as he was by what Jordan had done to Heather, he had to believe that the Jordan he loved was still inside that body and mind.

"There's a cot over there in the corner," said Jordan.

Zane's muscles were stiff from leaning over the worktable for so long. He'd built the bomb as slowly as possible. Twice Willis had ordered the guard to hit him for being too slow. He'd delayed as much as he could. He tried to come up with a way that would make the bomb look like it would work, but not be operational. But Willis knew enough about bomb building to catch him in that. Hiding the chemicals had been a last-ditch effort to create a bomb that wouldn't work.

Zane glanced up to where he was sure a camera was. He had no doubt that Willis was watching them. The underground bunker had only been a dream seven years ago. Willis must have been here since the spring to have time to build something like this.

Feeling defeated, Zane collapsed onto the cot. He knew if he spoke the microphones would pick it up. How could he reach Jordan?

Jordan pulled a chair across the floor. The scraping noise of metal on concrete made Zane cringe. Jordan sat in the chair. Still holding the gun, he crossed his arms.

Zane stared at him, hoping to force him to make eye contact.

Jordan glanced from side to side, deliberately not looking at Zane.

The room was especially warm. Zane took off his flannel shirt. His gaze fell to the tattoo on his arm, the one that said "Brothers are Forever." Jordan had the same tattoo. Zane crossed his arms and tapped the tattoo over and over.

It was hard to read emotion in Jordan through the thick hair and beard. Zane wasn't sure whether or not Jordan even noticed, but he didn't stop trying. He just kept tapping the tattoo. If Willis or one of the guards were watching, they probably wouldn't understand what he was doing.

Zane thought he saw some sort of emotion flicker across Jordan's face.

Jordan shifted in his chair, pointed the gun toward the floor and stared down the barrel. "Why don't you get some sleep?"

Jordan's back was to the camera. If he wanted to show some sign he got what Zane was doing, he could.

Jordan finally made eye contact. What Zane saw in Jordan's eyes was glacial.

A deep sadness sank in as he realized how lost his brother was. "What did Willis promise you? Some kind of promotion?"

Jordan looked to the side as if seeing some faraway scene through the wall. "Get some sleep. We need to get that bomb built."

Zane lay down and flipped over on the cot so he faced the wall. He closed his eyes but knew he wouldn't be able to sleep.

A moment later, he heard Jordan get up from his chair and stomp across the floor. He tapped on the trapdoor. It swung open on creaking hinges. Jordan shouted up at the other guard. "Hey, can you take over? I'm beat."

"Sure, man." Zane heard more stomping and the

door closing. The guard grunted as he sat down in the chair.

Zane made deep breathing noises so the guard would think he was sleeping. His mind was racing too fast for him to even close his eyes.

As soon as the bomb was finished, both he and Heather would be killed. They only had a few hours to live unless he came up with a way to escape.

Heather tore the cut rope off her wrists. The shed was small, maybe four foot square, made from one of those kits you could buy at a home-improvement store. She pushed on the door. It opened. That meant that there was probably a guard close by. She eased the door open just a bit and poked her head out. The large central bonfire still smoldered, but the men who had gathered around it earlier were gone. She heard snoring, but could see no movement anywhere. No sign of someone pacing with a rifle. She slipped outside, crouching and listening, waiting for her eyes to adjust to the light. She couldn't assume she'd just be able to walk through the camp. It might have been a trap to leave the shed unlocked. She had a fleeting moment of wondering if it *had* been locked and Nathan had come by and unlocked it when no one was looking.

As she was able to discern objects in the dark, she saw the source of the snoring—a man propped against a tree with a rifle resting across his lap. She skirted away from the guard.

Voices alerted her to two men walking by. She flattened herself against the ground, not even daring to breathe as their footsteps pounded past her. She could easily navigate to the bunker where Zane was by going through the camp, but there was risk of being seen.

She opted to head toward the forest, circle around the edge of the camp and try to find the bunker that way. She hurried through the trees running in the general direction of the bunker. But after a few steps, she stopped, confused. Had the bunker been this way? Or another way instead? There was nothing distinctive about the part of the forest where the bunker was. She could end up wandering around here until daylight, and then her opportunity to get Zane and escape the camp would be gone.

She feared, too, that the guard might wake up to check on her. Then the camp would go on full alert. She had to hurry.

Heather scurried as fast as she dared until she had a view of the camp. Several men sat by a smaller campfire talking in low tones and cleaning their rifles. Their backs were to her. Now she saw the trail that led to the bunker. She'd have to sneak past the men, coming close enough to be detected if she wasn't careful.

As she crouched by a bush, she watched. The men seemed engaged in their conversation. None of them lifted their heads or looked around.

She rose and sprinted for the cover of the next bush.

There was an eruption of loud noises at the other end of the camp. Adrenaline shot through her system. The men at the fire jumped to their feet and ran in the direction of the noise. She pressed low to the ground as they rushed by her.

Once they were out of earshot, she headed toward the trail running through the trees. She stayed to the side of it—she'd be too visible if she walked along the path—but kept the trail in sight. More men dashed by on the trail. Some sort of alarm had been sounded. Had they checked the shed and found out she was gone or was there some other disruption?

She hurried into the forest again. The eruption of voices increased and more men ran through the camp. The trail ended. Her gaze darted around. Panic threatened to make her shut down. Nothing looked familiar. Where was that trapdoor? She ran in one direction and then the other, remembering that a guard had been posted outside the door. She didn't see anyone. Had he already left to deal with the disruption on the other side of the camp? It didn't seem like a guard would abandon such an important post when there were plenty of other men to deal with the disturbance.

The noise on the other side of the camp grew louder. They were coming this way. She sprinted through the forest, frantic to find the trapdoor. Finally, she spotted trees that looked vaguely familiar. She ran back and forth in a zigzag pattern until her foot touched metal. She got down on her knees and brushed the tree boughs away. If there was still a guard inside, he would hear the door creak as it opened. She found a log, flipped open the door and stood back waiting for the guard to stick his head out.

She raised the log. Footsteps came her way.

The noise of the mob of men reached her ears. They were getting closer. They must be looking for her. The guard's footsteps sounded on the stairs. Sweat trickled down her back as she waited. She would only get one shot at this. His head emerged and she swung at him just before he turned and would have seen her. The guard crumpled to the ground. She pushed him aside and rushed down the stairs.

Zane leaped up from a cot as soon as he saw her. He ran across the room and grabbed his coat.

She felt suddenly dizzy when she entered the room as images of the torture she'd endured bombarded her.

Zane grabbed her arm. "You did good. Let's go."

White dots filled her field of vision.

"I'm sorry for what happened here. But I promise you were safe the whole time. There were no bullets in the gun." He squeezed her arm above the elbow and brushed his hand tenderly over her cheek.

He instinctually seemed to know how the room affected her. The comfort of being near him again made some of the panic recede. The spots cleared from her eyes, and she was able to follow him when he pulled her toward the open trapdoor. Once outside, she saw torches in the distance down the trail, men growing closer. They must be searching for her. They'd probably figured out she'd come to rescue Zane.

Zane pulled her toward the trees just as several men stepped into the clearing. They ran haphazardly through the forest. Branches brushed her head. She jumped over logs that seemed to loom up toward her in the dark. She kept her eyes on Zane's back as she gulped in air and willed her legs to move faster, be stronger. *Run, run, go.*

Zane darted even farther ahead of her. She heard a crackling and swooshing sound. Zane groaning. She caught up with him to find that Zane hung in a net suspended from the air. Willis's men must have set traps all over the forest.

She could hear the men approaching. She only had

seconds to free him. She pulled the pocketknife out. The torches shone through the trees as the shout of the men pounded on her ears.

She had to stretch her arms to reach the netting that held Zane captive.

"Heather, there's not enough time. Run. At least that way one of us will be free. They'll have no leverage against me to force me to finish the bomb if they don't have you."

She glanced over her shoulder. The men were breathing down her neck. But she wasn't ready to give up. "I can get you out." She reached up to cut a strand of the netting.

The noise of the pursuers pressed on her from all sides.

Zane's voice intensified. "Go."

She could hear the men as they pushed their way through the trees, drawing near.

She cut another strand of the netting. The men were within yards of finding them. Her face was very close to Zane's.

"Go," he whispered.

He was right. "I'll come back for you. I'll get you out."

"I know you will."

She dashed off into the darkness, praying to God she would be able to keep her promise to Zane.

THIRTEEN

Zane listened to Heather's retreating footsteps. The men came into the clearing. Jordan was with them.

"Spread out," Jordan said. "We need to find the girl."

The men ran in several different directions, leaving Jordan and one other man to get Zane out of the net. It tore Zane up inside to think of Heather out there alone in the cold night.

Zane tried to keep his tone light, still hoping to reach Jordan. "I forgot about all the traps, little brother."

Jordan didn't respond. Instead, he walked to where the release was for the netting and pulled it.

The impact of hitting the ground sent waves of pain through Zane's back. The other man tore the netting off Zane while he kept a gun pointed at him.

"This will have to be reset," said Jordan.

"I can get that done," said the second man.

Jordan pulled out his own gun, which had a light on it. He pointed it at Zane. "Let's get moving. You have a bomb to finish."

The image of his brother pointing a gun at him nearly broke Zane's heart. "Oh, Jordie," he said, shaking his head. His brother was the only blood he had. How had it gotten to this point?

In the limited light, he couldn't read his brother's response to his heartfelt cry. He thought he saw Jordan's shoulders slump, but was that just wishful thinking?

Jordan led him back to the bunker, then disappeared through the side door without even a backward glance. This time, the guard didn't shackle Zane to the wall. He stared at the nearly complete bomb in front of him before sliding down the wall and sitting. At least for now they had no way of making him finish the bomb.

A moment later, Willis and Jordan burst through the side door.

Willis crossed his arms and stood with his feet shoulder width apart. Jordan took up the same stance.

"I think it's time you complete your job," Willis ordered, jerking his chin up.

"I'm not building your bomb. I'm not participating in whatever destruction you have in mind."

Willis signaled the guard with a head nod. The guard marched across the concrete and pulled Zane to his feet. Zane braced to be hit or tortured or whatever they had in mind. He didn't care what they did to him.

The guard hit Zane in the back with the rifle. His knees buckled, and he grabbed the table for support. He offered Willis a glance that had steel in it.

"Kill me if you want. I'm not finishing that bomb." Zane spoke through gritted teeth.

The look of stone-cold indifference on Jordan's face hurt worse than the blow to his back.

Willis stared at Zane for a long moment before pulling his radio off his belt and saying something into it. A moment later, the trapdoor opened and another guard appeared.

Willis's blue eyes seemed to turn even icier under the cold fluorescent light. He kept his gaze on Zane while he spoke to the guards. "It seems Mr. Scofield here is not properly motivated to complete his job. What can we do about that?"

A long heavy silence descended in the room like a shroud.

Jordan crossed his arms and lifted his chin.

"What we need to accomplish here is so important for the future of our country, don't you agree, Jordan?"

Jordan nodded.

Willis continued, still not taking his eyes off Zane. "You've been my right-hand man for almost a year now, haven't you?"

Again Jordan nodded, though his gaze darted from one of the guards to the other and his forehead wrinkled. He didn't seem to know where this was going. That made two of them.

Willis walked over to the table where the gun they had used on Heather still lay. He opened the cylinder and pulled a bullet out of his pocket, put it in and spun the cylinder. He stared at the gun. "Yes, what Mr. Scofield needs is the proper motivation."

Zane straightened and placed his hands on his hips as a show of defiance toward Willis. Fine, Willis could play Russian roulette with him if he wanted to. He didn't care if he died; he wasn't going to have it on his conscience that a bomb he'd built was used in a crime to terrorize people and steal their prized possessions. He wouldn't be able to live with himself anyway.

Willis signaled both the guards. They moved in and

grabbed Jordan, forcing him to sit in the same chair Heather had sat in.

Jordan protested. The look in his eyes was wild.

Zane had seen that look when Jordan had been unfairly punished for something another kid had done in the boys' home they'd been placed in.

The two guards secured Jordan to the chair while he struggled to break free. The cry that came out of Jordan's mouth sounded almost childlike.

Watching Jordan resist made Zane feel like his own heart was being torn out. Willis had never cared about people. His own twisted goals meant more to him. Zane had figured that out once he was no longer under Willis's influence. But Jordan was clearly figuring that out for the first time. It had to be a harsh shock that Willis, the man Jordan looked up to and admired, saw him as expendable.

Once Jordan was restrained, Willis walked over to him. His boots pounded on the concrete. He raised the gun and pointed it at Jordan's temple, still staring straight at Zane.

"Do you feel properly motivated now?"

Zane could not tear his eyes away from Jordan. He was breathing through his teeth and sweat glistened on his forehead. The look of utter defeat in Jordan's eyes spoke volumes.

Zane stared down at the bomb components and then back up at Willis as he held the gun to Jordan's head. His brother might die, just when he'd started to see Jordan's loyalty cracking. This final act of betrayal may finally help Jordan see Willis for the selfish egomaniac he was, but it might be too late.

"Get to work," said Willis. He pulled the hammer back on the revolver.

If this bomb got built, a robbery would happen. Even if no one was hurt or killed in the robbery itself, Willis might end up using the money from the robbery and the pot farm to finance more destruction and even death.

"What exactly are you planning on doing with this?"

"Quit stalling." Willis shifted his weight and jammed the gun barrel against Jordan's temple.

Zane glanced at his brother, who looked like he'd completely fallen apart.

He couldn't let Jordan die. He'd have to find another way to stop the snowballing of this violence.

As he picked up the container that held the chemicals to create the bomb, he prayed that Heather had escaped and found a way back into camp. He would do everything he could to get out of here to prevent the disaster Willis had in mind, but he needed her help. The only way out of this was if they worked together. All his hope for a good outcome hung on that.

Heather entered the camp just as sunlight peeked through the trees. This time she had no problem finding the bunker. With all the chaos in chasing her and Zane, the branches to cover the entrance hadn't been replaced. Even better, a guard had not been put back on the trapdoor. It was not a safe way to enter the bunker though. They'd hear the door opening and have too much time to prepare as she came down the stairs. And there was probably at least one guard inside.

She remembered the side door where Willis had come from. Maybe there was a separate entrance.

She had to act fast. Men were still out looking for

her. She'd managed to throw them off the trail and double back, but it would be only a matter of time before they tracked her down.

She scanned the area around the trapdoor and looked up toward where Willis's cave was. Maybe there was a passageway between the cave and the bunker. That might be why Willis came through the side door.

After glancing over her shoulder, she hurried up toward the cave. No guard stood outside the entrance. She slipped inside, prepared to fight if she had to. A man slept in the corner with his back to her.

She tiptoed deeper into the cave. Light shone from one of the openings. Her chest squeezed tight. All of this might be a waste of precious time. The sleeping man started to roll over. She dashed toward the lit tunnel.

She hurried through the cool dampness of the cave. Battery-operated lights revealed the path she needed to take. As she rounded a corner in the tunnel, voices echoed. Whatever she was stepping into, it would be dangerous. Nathan was the only member of Willis's army who had not shown blind loyalty to Willis and he was probably gone by now.

The cold stone of the cave turned into wood. She stepped into an area filled with shelving that contained food, cleaning supplies, blankets, first-aid kits and boxes of bullets. The supplies someone might need to survive long-term.

The voices grew louder and more distinct as the distortion from the echo in the cave faded. Now she could discern Willis's voice.

She had no gun, no weapon at all but her pocketknife. She couldn't just enter the bunker. She stared at the shelves of food and supplies. She remembered from high school chemistry class that if she put sugar and the potassium nitrate from the cold packs in the first-aid kit together, she could create a smoke bomb. Maybe that would be enough of a distraction for her to get Zane out. She worked to gather the items and a container to hold them. She grabbed a box of matches.

The voices in the room next to her quieted. She tensed, fearing Willis would come stomping through at any moment. Her heartbeat drummed in her ears as her hands trembled. Once her smoke bomb was assembled, she eased toward the door. Silence seemed to press on her from all sides. What exactly was going on in that bunker?

She'd have only a moment to take in the scene before smoke from her bomb filled the room. She lit the matches that served as a fuse and held the bomb until it began to smoke.

Another voice floated into the room. "Please stop doing this to him. Doesn't his loyalty mean anything to you?" That was Zane's voice.

"Get back behind the table." Willis sounded nervous.

Zane must be making his move. Now was the moment. She pushed open the door and tossed the smoke bomb as she entered the room. Zane had come out from behind the table where the other bomb was being built.

She caught a flash of Jordan tied to a chair, his head hanging, hair covering his face. Was he dead? Willis turned to see her, a gun in his hand, just as the room filled with smoke. A gunshot reverberated through the concrete room. Zane found her hand in the smoke. She pulled him toward where she thought the door was.

Her hand touched solid wall. She reached for the door. Her fingers scraped over what felt like metal hinges. She lunged toward a break in the concrete. The smoke followed them into the supply room but dissipated enough that she could see where they were.

She pulled him through the room.

He stopped. "We have to get Jordan."

Willis kicked open the door and aimed the gun at Heather as the smoke cleared.

There was no time to go back now. She took off running, knowing that Zane would be right behind her. In the narrow enclosed storage room, the noise of the gunshot made her ears ring. The bullet must have pierced the food supplies because flour poured out of a bag above her and spilled onto the floor.

She hurried up to the cave, where the guard was now wide awake. Though he appeared surprised to see Heather, he lunged at her, reaching for her neck. Zane came up from behind and landed a blow to the guard's jaw just as he grabbed Heather.

The guard pounced on Zane and tackled him to the ground. Zane rolled across the cave floor, coming dangerously close to the fire. He managed to get on top of the guard and land several debilitating blows to the man's face and chest. Eventually the guard seemed to lose his will to fight. Zane got off him, breathing heavy and ready to jump into the battle again.

Flames shot up around the hem of Zane's coat.

Heather pointed. "Fire!"

Zane glanced down.

Though he still looked disoriented, the guard picked up a stick by the fire and raised it to whack Zane on the head. Heather charged toward the man from the side.

The move caught the man off guard. He stumbled sideways.

Zane ripped his coat off and stomped on the flames. The man recovered enough to lunge toward Zane with the stick still in his hand.

Heather jumped on his back and bit into his shoulder. The man yowled and tried to shake her off. Zane landed a blow to the man's stomach that doubled him over. Heather slipped off the guard's back.

"Come on, we don't have much time." Zane hurried toward the cave entrance.

Willis appeared at the other entrance.

They dashed out of the cave. Men rushed toward them from down below. Willis must have radioed ahead.

Panic flooded through Heather's awareness. "We can't go down there."

Zane headed up the mountain. A rifle shot bounced off a nearby rock. Heather froze. She could feel herself shutting down as her vision blurred. This was all too much. Zane turned and grabbed her hand.

"We've made it this far. Don't give up."

His voice was enough for her to shake the paralysis. They pushed up the mountain and over the other side. Wind rushed around her as they stood on the summit. Down below, several men were still snaking up the path toward them.

Zane rested his hand on her shoulder. "It looks like they're giving up."

She glanced down. The men had slowed their pace.

"The real danger will be at the bottom of the mountain on the other side. They can get around to there with their ATVs faster than we can get down. They'll be waiting to ambush us."

She tensed. "When will this stop?"

"We are witnesses, Heather. Willis is not going to let us out of the high country alive."

Her stomach tightened into a knot.

He grabbed her at the elbows and pulled her toward him. The look in his eyes intensified. "I know you want to give up. But hold on. Can you do that for me?"

She nodded, but felt as though her knees would buckle.

He drew her into his arms. "You're smart and strong. You got me out of that bunker. We can do this."

His arms enveloped her. She melted into the warmth of his embrace breathing in the scent of his skin. "I just don't see how."

He held her close. "There is more at stake than just you and me. A bank robbery is going to happen—they have the explosives to make it happen. I couldn't let Jordan die. I had to assemble the bomb."

She relished the strength she got from being held by him. "I know you did everything to prevent it, but I wish the bomb wasn't finished."

"It may be finished, but it won't work without this magnesium ribbon." Zane pulled what looked like a piece of metal out of his pocket.

"That will make him hunt us all the harder." Her voice faltered.

"This isn't just about us. I don't know what exactly Willis has planned, but we have to stop him," Zane said.

He was right. She'd seen firsthand that Willis was evil. "I have it on good authority that Willis is going to rob the safety deposit boxes in Fort Madison. Apparently, a rich man around here has recently put items of value in there."

Zane smoothed over his beard. "Makes sense. He likes to target low-security, rural banks like Fort Madison." He touched her elbow. "Let's keep moving."

Fear permeated every cell of Heather's body as she stared down the steep incline knowing that they were probably walking into an ambush and that they had no choice.

FOURTEEN

Zane worked his way down the steep mountainside with a heavy heart. He'd left his brother behind, even though Jordan might be in a different place now that Willis had betrayed him so horribly. Maybe now he'd be ready to leave Willis.

Heather stumbled on a rock as she ran beside him. He grabbed her arm at the elbow. He had to think of Heather. She'd risked her own life to save his. He wiped his mind clean of the pain thinking about his brother brought up. "You all right?"

She gave him a raised eyebrow look. "Just peachy."

He smiled despite their dire situation. "I appreciate the positive outlook."

He stared down the mountain. They could see most of the valley from this vantage point. Though he didn't see any men or ATVs yet, he knew it was just a matter of time.

"Is there some way we can avoid them?"

He picked up on the fear in her voice and wanted to say something comforting, but he couldn't lie to her. "The descent is treacherous, and there are only a few places where we would come out into the valley. I'm sure they will post guards at each of them."

She let out a breath and shook her head. "Are we anywhere close to getting out the way we had planned?"

He shook his head. "At this point, it would be faster to try to get out by the river."

He watched as she climbed. Her focus was on the rough terrain as she slanted her feet sideways to keep from slipping. Her long dark hair was still pulled back in a single braid. She'd been so brave and strong thus far. And this wasn't even her fight.

He gripped a rock and worked his way down, as well. What could he say to her that he hadn't already said? Holding her close had renewed his own strength and resolve. He wondered if she had felt the same way.

As they made their descent, he kept watch for signs that Willis was assembling forces below. He caught a glimpse of ATVs moving through the trees. He had to assume they were walking into a firefight.

Heather's feet slipped, and when she fell, she remained seated. He came up beside her and cupped his hand on her shoulder. The look on her face was of complete exhaustion.

"Rest a moment," he said.

She pulled her glove off and patted his hand. The warmth of her touch seeped through his skin.

She stared at the sky. "I know these men are dangerous. I know they need to be stopped."

She must be trying to find some inner resolve to keep going. He sat beside her, resting his elbows on his thighs.

She leaned against his shoulder.

"I wish there was an easy way out of this," he said.

He studied the valley below and the possible trails to get to the base of the mountain.

She covered his knee with her hand. "Me too."

"Your father used to tell me that the harder something was, the more worthwhile it would be in the end. That there was value in the struggle."

She caught him in her dark eyed gaze. "Sometimes I feel like when I look at you, I get a glimpse of my father. If he hadn't come into your life, you would have been like Jordan...so lost."

Sadness washed through Zane all over again and he hung his head. "I tried to get him out when I left. I really did." Maybe since Willis had used Jordan in such a horrible way, his brother might still be reached. He had to hold on to that hope.

She leaned closer and touched his back. "I didn't mean to upset you. I only meant to say you're such a good man, it must mean my father was, too, at the end of his life."

He turned to face her. Her brown eyes held a spark in the early-morning light. He felt drawn to her.

He rested his hand on her cheek, leaned in and kissed her. She responded. Her lips were like silk as he deepened the kiss.

He pulled back first, tracing the edges of her face with his fingers. Her expression brightened beneath his touch.

He wanted to stay in that moment forever, but down below, he heard the sounds of ATVs and caught a flash of color and movement.

"They're already getting into place," she said. Dread

tainted her words as the special moment between them gave way to reality.

They might not be able to avoid Willis's men altogether, but he could increase the odds that they would be able to escape. "We can come out where the ATVs can't go. Then we're just dealing with men on foot." He stood up and mentally scoped out the path they would take.

He hurried down the steep hillside, slipping a little. Heather was right behind him. She crashed against his back several times until they were in thick brush and could hold on to the trees for balance.

A rifle shot zinged over their head. Both of them ducked.

Zane studied the surrounding hills until he saw the glint of glass reflecting the sun. Willis had put a sniper in place. Anytime they were in the open, they'd be easy to pick off. Both he and Heather were targets now. Willis didn't need Zane alive anymore. He just needed the magnesium strip, and the men could take that off Zane's dead body. He thought to simply toss it away, but decided it might buy them leverage if they were caught.

"Every time the terrain opens up, stay low and move slow." The camo they both wore would give them a degree of cover, but a really good sniper knew what to look for. "Put your gloves in your pockets. They make you too easy to see."

They worked their way down the steep mountainside until they came to an open area covered with rocks. The camo wouldn't do them any good here.

"Move as fast as you can and stay as close to the brush as you can get," he said.

"Why not just go into the brush?"

"Too thick. Too treacherous." The tangled junipers and other brush would be impossible to navigate through.

Heather took the lead, dashing across the rocks, choosing the larger ones for cover. The first shot hit a stone right in front of Zane. His heart skipped a beat but he kept running.

Heather was within ten yards of cover when another rifle shot sliced through the air. She went down.

His heart seized up as he hurried toward her, expecting to see a pool of blood seeping out from beneath her. Another shot came close to his head. He couldn't get to her without being a target himself. He dived behind a large rock and poked his head around it. She still wasn't moving.

"Heather." His voice cracked.

She turned her head to face him. "I'm all right. Just lost my courage."

Relief spread through him. For a moment, he'd seen his life without her, how empty it would be.

She offered him a faint smile before rising and bolting for the cover of the trees. He looked across the landscape to where the sniper was positioned. Then Zane jumped to his feet and made a mad dash for the cover of the trees.

The sniper probably had the best spotting equipment money could buy. He might even have a spotter helping him. Even if he couldn't get a clean shot off, he would be able to track them down the mountain.

Though he kept his pessimism to himself, he wasn't real hopeful about their chances of making it to the bottom alive.

* * *

Heather was out of breath as she pushed her way through the thick brush.

Zane came up behind her, placing his palm on her back. "Wait." He studied the area in front of him. "We're almost to the base of the mountain. Let's go horizontal until we can find a good place to exit."

She knew he was looking for potential ambushes. The more treacherous the path they came out on, the less likely it was that they would be caught.

Zane stopped and crouched low, peering through the trees. The brush was so thick she could only see a few feet in front of her. She pressed close to him and listened. Branches creaked in the wind. A crow cawed from a distant tree.

She didn't hear or see anything that suggested Willis's men were lying in wait. If they were there, would they eventually grow nervous and impatient and start to talk? Or would they remain hidden and silent, weapons drawn, watching for any movement?

Zane signaled for her to keep moving. He made an abrupt turn and headed toward the base of the mountain, running in a serpentine pattern to stay in the cover of the brush.

She could see the base of the mountain and the forest beyond. Zane came to where the brush ended and crouched. He must have studied every tree, trying to discern movement.

Finally, he signaled for her to step out. She followed behind him. Her gaze darted everywhere. It felt like an elephant was sitting on her chest as her ears tuned into all the sounds around her.

She tried to take in a deep breath. As the landscape leveled off and opened up, Zane broke into a trot. She ran beside him, still expecting to be attacked. Every once in a while, he'd stop and study the landscape and look at the sky.

Her hands grew cold. She slipped her gloves on while she kept running.

She watched the trees for any sign of movement or flash of color. Still nothing. It didn't seem possible that they had outwitted Willis's men. But gradually the fear of getting caught was overwhelmed by other concerns. She was exhausted and hungry. And it was cold enough that she could see her breath. Zane ran shoving his bare hands into his pockets from time to time.

She stopped and pulled her gloves off. "Here, we'll take turns."

He put the gloves on. They ran through the day. Gradually the terrain started to look familiar. She recognized the mountain peak, the place where she was supposed to spread her father's ashes. The slim wooden box still pressed against her rib cage.

Clouds covered the sun. "Let's build a small fire and get warmed up," said Zane.

They gathered tinder and wood and chose a place where the trees surrounded them so the fire wouldn't be easy to spot.

She made a seat of dry evergreen boughs, sat and crossed her arms, mesmerized by the flames. Her legs ached from having run for days. And her empty stomach growled.

Zane found a plastic pop container that a hunter must have dropped or littered on purpose. He cut off the top, washed it with snow and then melted snow in it so they had something to drink. They passed the container back and forth, both of them staring at the fire.

"Why haven't they come for us?"

Zane scooted close to her. "We may have outwitted them. He might have only put a few men at the base of the mountain. My guess is that Willis positioned his men at all the points we might use for escape. That means his forces are spread pretty thin. Maybe two or three guys at each post."

"So if we try to cross the river at that other bridge to get back to Fort Madison, he'll probably have men waiting for us there?" She shivered, not from the cold but from the possibility of another battle.

"We have to cross the river. From where we are at now, it's the fastest way out."

She knew he was right.

Zane rubbed his beard with his hand. "Here's what I think we should do. They're expecting us to try to cross at one of the bridges. So I say we make a raft and just float down into Fort Madison."

Make a raft? Was he light-headed from exhaustion? "The only tool we have is my pocketknife."

"I know. And we'll have to come up with something to lash the poles together. If we can't make something seaworthy, we won't do it. But it's an option we need to consider."

Despair sank into her bones. Had it come to this unrealistic idea? She let out a heavy breath. "It just seems time and energy consuming. Aren't you wilderness guys always weighing energy expenditure against results and outcomes?"

"And you know this because—" There was a note of amusement in his voice.

"The survival shows on Discovery Channel."

Zane laughed. "Okay, so maybe my head isn't working right due to a lack of food. What do you suggest?"

She stared at the fire. Her stomach growled. "We need sleep and food and weapons."

"Stopping to rest is out of the question. Willis's men have the only weapons and food nearby. Are you saying we should ambush them?"

The thought made her stomach squeeze tight. "Some of the guys with him are just boys. They might have food on them and weapons for sure. If we get the chance, we should try."

Zane raised his head, brushing both hands over his beard. "Willis used to leave stashes of food and sometimes weapons buried or high up in the trees in case we were ever attacked. They'd be marked in a unique way. I forgot all about that."

Now she felt like they were getting somewhere. "So what were the markings like?"

"Something from nature, but out of place all the same. Roots braided together and hung on a tree or a ring of dried leaves. He might still be doing that."

A tree branch cracked not too far from them. Both of their backs straightened as they lifted their heads. Zane rose to his feet and kicked snow on the tiny fire. "Could be nothing but let's not take any chances."

She stood up, studying the trees section by section. Her heart drummed past her ears. "What if it's someone we could overpower?"

He tugged on her sleeve. Another noise—this one more distinctly human, a grunt—made them both take off running.

As they ran, she could hear the man or men behind

her charging toward them. Her tired leg muscles burned with pain. Still, she kept up with Zane as they jumped over fallen timber and angled through narrow spaces between the trees.

The pursuer never closed in on them but remained close enough that stopping and hiding wasn't an option.

She could feel herself slowing down and weakening. Zane decreased his pace, as well. One of the men was almost on top of them. They'd come this far and gotten this close; she wasn't about to give up. Both of them sped up to put more distance between them and the man or men chasing them.

When they could no longer hear their pursuer, Zane dived behind a log and flattened out. She scooted close to him. Her breathing sounded unbelievably loud.

She heard the footsteps of their pursuer as he ran through the trees past the log. Was it really just one guy out by himself? It seemed like Willis always sent the men and boys out in pairs.

"He might come back," Zane said. "We should try to take him. Grab a rock and climb a tree. Hurry."

With some effort she found a tree whose boughs would shield her from sight. Zane chose a tree not too far from her and climbed up. The minutes ticked by. She heard noise off to the side deeper in the trees. Maybe their pursuer had gotten sidetracked.

She heard a different man approaching, walking much slower. Heather took in a breath and prepared to be the attacker instead of the attacked.

FIFTEEN

Zane held the rock, ready to drop it. A tremendous crashing and breaking of branches coming from a different direction alerted him. An elk moved into his field of vision. Even from this angle, the animal was huge and magnificent. Its hooves pounded the earth as it thundered across the terrain. When it left the clearing, the area seemed even more silent.

A moment later, a teenage boy holding a bow stepped through the forest. One of Willis's followers, no doubt, hunting out of season. There were other things taking place besides chasing down Heather and Zane. The men relied heavily on the wild game they hunted. Zane realized even if the kid did come near the tree, he couldn't drop the rock on him.

These boys and young men were not truly evil, though they had been taught to do evil things just to stay alive or avoid Willis's wrath. They were lost just like he had been. Just like Jordan was.

He watched as the kid moved stealthily through the trees and decided that ambushing him would be pointless. The bow wouldn't be much of a weapon anyway. If they were going to face Willis's men at the river, they needed a gun. The bow hunter disappeared into the thick of the forest.

Once he was sure the bow hunter was gone, he dropped his rock on the ground. "Let's head toward the river. That kid was chasing down the elk, not us. If we do get a chance to jump one of them who has a gun and not kill him, we should take it."

Heather climbed down, dropping the last five feet to the ground. They hurried through the trees for at least half an hour. A smell filled the forest. Zane recognized that coppery taste in his mouth. They were getting close to a fresh game kill.

Heather put her hand over her nose. "What is that odor? Is it…a body?"

He picked up on the fear in her voice. "Yes, but it's not human." Zane made his way through the trees until he came to where the elk carcass lay. The bow hunter had worked fast. The animal was already dressed out and the hunter was gone. The teenager was on foot with no means of transporting the fresh meat before it spoiled. That meant he must have radioed for more men to come this way to pick it up.

The bow hunter had probably already moved on to try to get more game before the day was over.

"Let's get out of here." Zane tugged on Heather's sleeve. He heard noises to the side of him. He crouched behind some brush and Heather pressed in beside him.

Three young men wearing backpacks ran past them. One of them stopped to check his compass. "It's around here somewhere. Hurry."

These men were not after Heather and Zane. They were the cleanup crew for the elk. Less experienced and probably not fully trained to fight. He turned toward Heather. They could probably take one of the boys and get a weapon with no one being hurt. She nodded, showing she understood.

They leaped to their feet and fell in behind where the teenagers had just run. He could see that at least two of them had guns. They needed to wait for the chance when one of them was far enough away from the others to be vulnerable.

The boys' rapid pace slowed as they seemed to have lost their sense of direction. One of them checked the compass again. "I think we've gone too far. Let's split up. A hundred paces in different directions. Holler when you find it."

Zane dipped behind some brush, splitting off from Heather so they could come at the kid approaching their direction from either side.

Once he was in the cover of the trees, the kid slowed down and walked more aimlessly.

Zane caught a flash of movement through the trees that told him where Heather was. The kid stopped, placed his pistol on the ground and leaned over to tie his tennis shoe.

Heather ran ahead, bursting through the trees. She grabbed the gun and pointed it at the kid. "I don't want to hurt you."

The kid held up his hands. "My friends will be coming back this way."

Zane stepped into the clearing after her just as the kid whistled—probably some sort of signal for the other two. "We don't want to kill anyone today. That was never the plan."

A moment later, the other two young men appeared

on the opposite end of the clearing. One of them raised a rifle and pointed it in their direction.

Heather kept the gun steadily pointed at the first boy even as she said, "I really don't want to have to shoot anyone today."

Zane raised his hands in surrender. "We just need the gun."

The young man aimed the rifle at Zane and then at Heather. But his hands weren't steady, and those were not the eyes of a killer. He was afraid. That didn't mean he wouldn't impulsively pull the trigger though, which made him just as dangerous.

"We really need to get out of here." Tension threaded through Heather's words.

Zane called out, "If you'll just let us back off..." He turned his head sideways and spoke to Heather in a low voice. "Take a step back."

Heather continued to look down the sight as she backed up.

Zane pointed. "Your elk is off that way about thirty paces. If you don't get to it quickly it will spoil, and then you'll be in trouble."

The kid still twitched between aiming the gun at Zane and at Heather. The second young man only had a knife. Just as they slipped back into the trees, the second kid pulled out a radio and spoke into it. Great. Now that they'd been located, Willis's whole army would descend on them.

Both of them rushed through the thick forest. Zane directed their route toward the river.

Heather stopped, speaking in between breaths. "You should take the gun, since you're the better shot."

She met his gaze momentarily. There was a weightiness in her stare. "I couldn't shoot that kid. It was a total bluff."

"I know." The last thing he wanted to see was one of those boys die. Looking at them was like looking in a mirror at himself seven years ago. Willis was the bad guy here. All these kids deserved some kind of chance at a normal life and maybe a father figure who didn't attach conditions to his affection or make them fear his wrath.

They ran out into open, flat country, the sound of the river growing more prominent. Within minutes, they heard ATVs roaring across the landscape, becoming louder and closer.

The river came into view, a welcome sight. They hurried downhill to the steep, brush-populated bank.

"Let's get down there. It's a little narrow, but it gives us some cover."

Heather held out a hand for balance as she descended. The roar of the water filled his ears when he climbed down behind her. The path between the steep bank and the river was extremely narrow. They held on to the brush and balanced on a ledge no more than a few inches wide.

The dark, foaming water rushed over rocks and pushed debris downstream at a rapid pace. He'd already experienced the freezing chill of the river once and had no desire to live through that again.

Heather slipped and her toe dipped into the water. He caught her elbow.

"I'm all right," she said.

This close to the river the temperature dropped several degrees. They worked their way along the narrow bank. Though the sounds of the ATVs indicated that they were still not in the clear, the pattern of noise and the way it grew louder and then fell away indicated that the searchers were still cutting a wide swath to find them.

If they were found out, they would be like fish in a barrel. Although he was sure that Willis had ordered the men to retrieve the missing bomb component, the men wouldn't be foolish enough to shoot in such a way that Zane fell in the river and floated away with it.

They made progress inch by inch on the narrow pathway. The wind picked up a bit and his hands turned colder and stiff since he couldn't put them in his pockets for warmth. He needed to use them to balance. The shoreline opened up into rocky beach that allowed them to walk without risk of falling into the river.

The beach curved around. Zane slowed his pace. Up ahead he could see that several men were camped out where access to the river was easy. He and Heather were shielded from view by a rock formation.

"What do we do now?"

"We have to get back up on the bank and circle around them."

They started their ascent just as the sky turned a dusky gray. Once he was back on level land, Zane lay flat in the short grass and watched the men. There were three of them and they'd built a fire. Every ten minutes or so, one of them picked up a rifle and paced out a big circle. They must have been positioned here for some time. Their posture and lack of attention to their surroundings suggested boredom rather than vigilance. But Zane knew that all that apathy would switch to violence if they saw Heather or him.

Heather stayed close to Zane. Zane pointed at the

trees and then crawled commando style toward them. Several times, he glanced in the direction of the men to make sure no alarm bells had gone off for them.

Once they reached cover, they got to their feet and sprinted away from the river. A shout to the side of them told him they'd been spotted. Once the alarm was sounded, the forest seemed to come alive with pursuers. The ATVs were on top of them within minutes.

He and Heather ran as fast as they dared, forced to go through a part of the forest that had been burned by fire. They wouldn't find much cover in this part of the forest and the camo did them no good. The noise of men on the move seemed to surround them. Had they come all this way only to lose?

He'd run until he had no breath left. He was pretty sure Heather would do the same. He heard the barking of a dog, and it was like a blow to his gut. This was not going well. He prayed even as he sprinted and skirted around another burned tree.

God, please help us.

The noise of the pursuers seemed to surround them on three sides. Zane made a beeline toward where the forest had been unaffected by the fire. Though he was relieved to reach an area where the evergreens hid them from view, they weren't safe yet. They kept running. Zane wasn't sure how they were going to get away. He felt the fatigue in his own body. These men had had time to rest and refuel. He and Heather had not.

All the same, they kept a steady pace through the evergreens.

Jordan stepped into the clearing in front of them.

Both of them stopped.

Jordan had a gun in his holster but it wasn't drawn.

"Come with me, I can get you out of here."

Zane's throat went dry. Was his brother telling the truth or was this a trap?

Heather could feel her cheeks flush and her heart race at the sight of the man who had held a gun to her head. Clearly, this was a setup. She turned on her heel to run away.

Zane caught her by the elbow. "I think he's telling the truth. A lot happened back at that bunker."

The baying of the dog grew louder and closer.

"We don't have much time," said Jordan.

Heather couldn't shake her confusion. Jordan still looked wild eyed.

"This way." Jordan took off running.

Zane pulled Heather along even as she wrestled with uncertainty. Zane was Jordan's brother. Maybe he saw something she couldn't see. All she knew of Jordan was his violence and his loyalty to Willis at all costs.

The dog was so loud it sounded like it was at their heels. The forest grew denser. The trees were close enough together that it slowed their progress. Heather glanced over her shoulder. She could still hear the dog but not see it.

Jordan patted Zane on the shoulder and pointed. "Go on up ahead. I'll catch up with you."

They hurried through the thick grove of barren aspen trees.

Heather jogged as she spoke. "How do we know he's not leading us into a trap?"

Zane pushed through the trees staring straight ahead. "Things happened. I think Jordan's becoming disillusioned with Willis."

Was Zane seeing that in his brother because it was true or because it was what he so desperately wanted?

The barking of the dog grew farther away. Jordan must have pointed the searchers in a different direction. A few minutes passed and Jordan came running through the trees. "I've thrown them off for now. Come this way."

Jordan led them through the forest.

Heather felt a tightness in her chest. Where was Jordan taking them? He must know that Zane had the bomb component. If that was all he wanted, he could just shoot them. As far gone as Jordan had seemed, maybe even *he* couldn't shoot his brother. Could that small piece of humanity be left inside of him?

Her anxious thoughts tumbled one over the other. Finally, she planted her feet. "Where are you taking us?"

Jordan turned toward her. She thought she saw a flare of anger in his eyes. "We've only got a few minutes before that dog picks up the trail again. We need to keep moving."

Zane squeezed her hand and then took off running. She chose to follow even as she battled uncertainty. The grove of aspens ended, and they stepped toward a rocky incline. Jordan climbed with ease up the incline. Heather held out a hand and gripped a jagged rock. Jordan hadn't asked for Zane's gun. Maybe he did intend to help them.

A chill ran down her spine when she thought of the gun pressed against her temple and the coldness she'd seen in Jordan's eyes. She wanted to believe they weren't being set up. All the same, fear made it hard for her to keep going.

The rocky area leveled off. She glanced down below,

where she saw several men and the dog headed up the same winding trail they were on.

"They're gaining on us."

Jordan and Zane's response was to walk faster. Heather fought to keep up on the narrow trail. The brush was thick enough down below that she could only see their pursuers in quick flashes, which meant the pursuers wouldn't have a clear view of them either.

The barking of the dog intensified.

"They're getting too close," she shouted up ahead.

Jordan turned and lurched toward Heather. She took a step back as her heart pounded against her rib cage. He grabbed her at the elbows, sending shock waves of fear through her. Zane came toward them.

In his usual gruff manner, Jordan pulled Heather toward him and then pushed her in Zane's direction. "Take her and hide up there behind those rocks. Hurry."

Zane gathered her into his arms, but her panic levels were still high from having been manhandled by Jordan.

Zane whispered in her ear, "It's going to be okay."

She wasn't so sure about that. A man didn't change years of ingrained thinking in a few days.

They slipped behind the rocks, shoulders pressed close together, just as their pursuers arrived.

She could catch only bits and pieces of what Jordan said to the group of searchers, but it sounded like he was rerouting them and suggesting they go in a different direction because of what he had seen.

One of the men in the group seemed to protest Jordan's order.

Jordan raised his voice to shouting level. "What I say goes."

The dog continued to bark excitedly.

Zane leaned close to her as the wind buffeted around them. His hand slipped into hers. She had no idea what Jordan was up to, but she knew she could trust the man who crouched beside her. They waited for a long moment as the barking of the dog faded.

Jordan popped his head around the rock. "Come on, hurry."

Why did Jordan insist that they simply follow him blindly? Why couldn't he explain what he had in mind, where he was taking them?

Fear gripped her heart.

Jordan led them up another incline without saying anything more. He stopped midway down the other side of the mountain and looked around.

Heather turned nervously from one side and then to the other, half expecting armed men to emerge through the trees.

Jordan walked over to a distinctive white rock and then counted out ten paces before dropping to his knees. He turned and looked at Zane. "Give me a hand here."

Jordan started to clear away rocks and debris from a flat area. Zane knelt beside his brother and began to help. So did Heather. Gradually a steel plate came into view.

Jordan pulled a knife off his belt, flicked it open and used it to twist a dial on the steel plate. Jordan pushed the plate open and pulled out a bag. He tossed what looked like packets of food toward Heather and Zane. "Take this GPS." He threw a small velvet bag in their direction. "There are coordinates programmed into it that will take you the high point on the mountain range above the river. You'll find a stash of paragliding equipment there. Flying over that river is the only way you can avoid Willis."

Jordan closed the lid to the steel box and screwed it shut. All of them worked again to cover it with leaves and dirt. Once they were finished, they stood. Jordan patted his brother on the shoulder. "I need to get out of here before I'm missed."

Zane leaned toward his brother as though to give him a hug. Jordan stepped away, turned and disappeared down the trail.

Heather let out a breath, not sure what to think or believe.

Zane opened the bag with the GPS device and then studied the mountain. "We'd better get moving. We have about half a day's hike ahead of us."

"Do you think he's telling the truth?"

"We don't have a lot of choice here, Heather." A tone of defensiveness colored Zane's words. He skirted past her and took off walking.

She startled when she heard a rustling in the forest.

Zane came up beside her, drawing a protective arm across her back and cupping her shoulder. "Wild animal, maybe. Just keep moving."

They continued on the trail at a little quicker pace, running single file on the narrow path. Suddenly, two men jumped out on the path in front of them. Each held a gun.

They turned to run in the other direction.

Two more armed men stepped out onto the trail, blocking their path of escape.

Behind those two men stood Willis. "Well, well, well…what have we here?"

SIXTEEN

Zane could not believe what he was seeing. The emotional devastation nearly made him drop to his knees. They'd been surrounded—as if Willis had known their location all along. Had his brother betrayed him? At the core of his being, he didn't want to believe that was true.

Willis rubbed his buzz cut and stroked his clean-shaven jaw. "I think you have something I need."

Zane's thoughts felt muddled. He couldn't let go of what Jordan had done. Was it really possible? But he knew he had to push those feelings aside to focus on the danger of their situation. Once Willis got the magnesium strip, both he and Heather would be shot.

One of the men holding a rifle leaned close to Willis. "You want me to search him?"

Willis waved his hand. "I am sure Mr. Scofield will give me what I want of his own free will."

Willis could just shoot them both and search his lifeless body for the component. With Willis, though, everything was about domination and control. And right now he wanted Zane to surrender the strip and admit he was beaten.

The back of Heather's hand brushed his, then she slanted her gaze down the mountainside.

"You win, Willis." Zane shot her a quick look and then reached inside his jacket as though to pull something out.

With all eyes—and guns—pointed at Zane, Heather leaped off the trail and down into the thick trees. Zane followed. A few seconds passed before the gunfire started. The abundance of narrow lodgepole pine provided them with a degree of cover, though the mountainside was so steep they were practically sliding down. Would the men follow them into the treacherous terrain or run on the trail and try to meet up with them at the bottom?

His guess was that Willis would split his forces. Two down the steep mountainside and two on the trail.

The hillside became so steep that both he and Heather sat down and slid rather than trying to run, braking with their hands to keep from going too fast. A gunshot broke up the dirt close to his feet. When he glanced over his shoulder, he saw movement through the trees.

They continued to slide until the trail came back into view. Both of them jumped to their feet and started running. He heard shouting behind them. Another gunshot ricocheted off a tree close to Heather. She grabbed his arm. Her eyes were filled with fear. He patted her upper arm trying to reassure her. "Just keep going."

Their feet pounded the trail as they struggled to move faster.

The trail lengthened out into a long straightaway. The men were only twenty yards behind them. He and Heather headed back into the thick of the woods. The mountainside was not as steep here, but it was still way more treacherous than the trail.

Heather's foot caught beneath a root. She fell forward. Zane reached out and caught her, but the fall had cost them precious seconds. One of the men stepped out, aiming his gun at them.

He and Heather turned to head up the mountain into thick cover of the forest, but the second man stepped through the trees aiming his gun at them, as well.

The second man said, "Put your hands in the air. You best be heading down to the trail."

Both Zane and Heather complied. Zane's heart still raced from exertion and adrenaline. He fought off the impending sense that they were defeated and without hope. There had to be a way out. There had to be a way to stop Willis.

One of the men walked a few paces away and spoke into a radio. The man who was left to guard them looked like he was fairly young, maybe in his early twenties. His beard was splotchy and his eyes darted around nervously. His white eyebrows contrasted with his red hair.

"Can I put my hands down?" Heather said. "I'm getting tired."

The redheaded man nodded. "Just don't try anything."

Heather let her arms fall. Zane did the same. The man on the radio stopped talking and turned to face them again, aiming the gun at Zane. The redhead had his gun on Heather.

They waited for what seemed like an eternity. And then footsteps sounded on the trail above them.

From behind, they heard applause. And then Willis's voice. "A valiant effort. I taught you well, Zane. Just like I taught your brother."

The last comment was intended to cut through Zane's heart. The possibility that his brother had betrayed him weakened him even more.

"Both of you turn around and face me."

They turned slowly. Rage boiled to the surface when he saw the smirk on Willis's face, but Zane held it in check. Any sort of outburst could be deadly.

Willis held out his hand. "So, I think you have something I want."

Zane didn't move. His mind reeled, struggling to find a solution, but with three guns trained on them at close range, there was no way out that he could see.

Willis shook his head and made a tsking noise. "Not going to give it up, huh?"

Willis signaled the older of the two men, who opened his revolver and emptied it of all the bullets but one. He then dived and grabbed Heather by the hair, pushing her to the ground. She cried out when her knees impacted with the hard packed dirt of the trail. The man raised the gun to the back of Heather's head.

Zane's heart lurched. "I'll give it to you."

They were going to die anyway. Heather didn't need to go through the torture of roulette again.

"Very good," said Willis.

"It's in my inside pocket. I'll have to unzip it."

"I'm waiting," said Willis.

Zane reached inside his coat. He had a thought that he could just pull the strip out and toss it down the mountain. But once the strip was gone, he and Heather were dead. And there was too much risk the men would still be able find it.

His fingers grazed over the GPS device Jordan had led them to. Willis had not asked for the device. Did that mean he didn't know about it? Maybe Zane would die here today, but he refused to believe that his brother had betrayed him. Maybe Willis had been tracking them for some time and Jordan had had nothing to do with it.

He reluctantly handed over the component to Willis. Willis didn't even make eye contact as he walked away and barked orders at the two men. "I have a schedule to keep. We need to be in town by tomorrow morning." He put the component in his pocket. "I have no more need for these two. Do away with them." He cupped the shoulder of the redheaded man. "Earn your stripes."

Willis trotted down the trail, rounded a curve and disappeared.

Both men looked at each other. The older one only had one bullet in his gun, and the younger one didn't look like he could kill a rabbit.

"Turn around and get on the ground by your girl-friend," said the older man. Heather lifted her head to look at Zane.

This could not be the end for them. There had to be a way out. The older man opened the cylinder of his revolver to reload it, reaching into his pocket for the bullets.

Zane stepped as though he were going to move to-ward Heather but instead lunged at the redheaded man, punching him in his face and stomach. Zane grabbed the man's gun and turned it on the older man.

"You'd have to close the cylinder before you could fire, and with only one bullet, you'd have no way of knowing if it's the next one in the chamber."

The man held up his hands.

"Drop the gun."

He complied.

Heather hurried to pick up the discarded gun. She held out her hand. "Give me the other bullets."

The man dug into his jeans' pockets and slammed them into Heather's hand.

"Both of you on your knees, facing away from me."

"What are you going to do to us?" Fear permeated the redhead's voice.

Zane leaned close and said, "I'm not the animal Willis is." He knocked both men on the side of the head with the butt of the gun.

"Are they going to be okay?"

"They'll wake up shortly. And then I'm sure they'll come after us and bring reinforcements." He took the radio off the man and tossed it down the mountain. "You heard Willis. He's planning on hitting that bank in the morning."

He took off running up the trail.

"Where are we going?" She was out of breath as she spoke and jogged at the same time.

He turned to face her and patted the pocket where the GPS device was. "Willis didn't know about this. He didn't try to take it away from me."

"You think Jordan was telling us the truth. That he didn't set us up to be ambushed."

"It's the only shot we have. We've got to stop Willis from detonating that bomb."

Heather's forehead wrinkled. "What if we get to the place where the paragliders are supposed to be and they're not there? We will have wasted all our time on a fantasy."

His mind had been mulling over everything that had happened since Willis was able to find them so easily on the trail. Maybe Jordan had chosen to help his brother but still intended to stay with Willis. That possibility broke his heart. Was his mind so brainwashed that he'd stay loyal to Willis no matter what?

Zane shook his head. "This is our only option. We have to hope that Jordan was telling the truth."

Zane turned on his heel and ran, knowing that Heather would follow. He knew approximately where the high point on the mountain was that Jordan had referenced. They'd have to dip down into a valley and then climb up to the summit, a four- or five-hour hike if they kept up a good pace.

He glanced over his shoulder and slowed a little allowing Heather to catch up. The trail widened so they could run side by side. He could see only trees above him—very little light sneaked through this late in the day. Down below, he could still see some of Willis's men who had been part of the hunt. They weren't coming after him and Heather for the moment—but that would change as soon as the two men he'd knocked out woke up and shared the news that their would-be victims had turned the tables and escaped. Zane feared that someone would be waiting to jump them at the top of the trail as well.

After they'd rounded several curves and the men were no longer in sight, he stopped and pointed up through the forest. "We can't stay on this trail. They'll start looking for us here soon. There might even be men at the top."

She rested her hands on her hips, breathing heavily from the exertion of running. Both of them stared at the evergreens and steep hill that intersected with the winding trail.

"The trees will at least hide us from view," he said.

They pushed through the steep terrain, gripping the trees and brush to make it up.

He sat down to catch his breath and Heather sat beside him.

"We're almost to the top. If men were signaled that we were headed this way, they'll be looking for us but expecting us to come out on the trailhead."

Heather nodded.

"You might want to put those bullets in your gun now," Zane suggested.

She pulled the bullets from her pocket and clicked open the cylinder, placing the rounds in one by one. She clicked it back in place and put the gun in her pocket with the safety on.

They pushed silently through the trees until they had a view of the ridgeline. Zane surveyed the trees and the brush for any movement.

He crawled a little farther up, still watching. They used the shelter of the trees, walking parallel to the trail. His heart pounded out a wild rhythm as he braced for an attack.

The trees thinned, and they stepped out into the open. The wind was more intense without the shelter of the trees. They were on what was nothing more than a game trail. For the moment, they seemed to be alone.

Zane pointed out the route they needed to take. "We'll dip down into that valley and then climb up to the summit there."

Heather let out a heavy breath. "That's a long way."

It would be dark by the time they made it...*if* they

made it. "Once we get up to the summit, we'll be able to see the river on the other side.

"Let's eat the food Jordan gave us and then we'll have to run as much as we can." He glanced around again, still not seeing any signs of Willis's men.

They settled in with their backs against a fallen log. The only noise was the sound of their chewing.

"I hope you're right about Jordan," Heather said. "Not just so we can have a chance of getting into town, but because he's your brother." She placed her hand on his.

Zane squeezed his eyes shut. Willis had influenced Jordan at a very impressionable age. That sort of brainwashing didn't get erased instantly. "I hope I'm right, too. We'd better shove off. We've got a lot of ground to cover." He rose to his feet and turned to face Heather. "This wasn't your battle to fight. All this violence is because of me and my past. But you stuck with me without complaining." He touched his hand to her cheek.

Heather placed her hand over his. "I wouldn't have it any other way. I know now that my father must have been an extraordinary man—because you are. You must have learned it from him, just like Jordan learned violence from Willis."

He thought he saw the glow of affection in her eyes. Could there be something between them? Maybe if they got out of here alive and their lives calmed down. "It does matter who your fatherly influence is."

"My father's faith must have been deep because yours is. Makes me wish I had that kind of faith."

"How do you know you don't? Maybe it's just never been tested," Zane said.

A light came into her eyes and she nodded. "You might be right. I know I've never prayed before like I have since all of this started."

They were both aware of the peril and risk they faced. There was still a chance Jordan had lied to them. They might not get off this mountain alive. Maybe that was what compelled them to speak so honestly.

He brushed his hand over her forehead and down her cheek. "We'd better get moving."

They stepped out onto the ridgeline and headed down into the valley at a steady jog.

Within minutes, men emerged through the trees, coming at them from both sides and at a high rate of speed—two men from the east and one from the west.

Zane and Heather ran faster through the snow-laden valley as the men closed in on them. Heather pressed close to him as he pumped his legs, willing them to go faster.

One of the men raised a gun to shoot at them. Zane grabbed hold of Heather and plummeted to the ground as the bullet whizzed over their heads. The snow was cold on his bare hands. He rose to his feet and helped Heather up.

They headed toward the shelter of the trees just as the men converged on them. They pushed through the trees with the men twenty yards behind them.

Zane studied the trees, looking for the markers that indicated traps had been set. He saw the subtle indicators that only expert eyes would notice. Notches in a tree, a piece of faded fabric tied to a branch. Maybe the old traps were still here and maybe these men didn't know about the older traps.

He ran in the direction he thought a net might be. The men were within forty feet of them.

He wrapped an arm around Heather and pulled her close when she nearly stepped on the trigger for the net. The men closed in on them. One of them raised his gun. Zane dashed out of the line of fire, hoping the men would follow him. Their pursuers ran through the clearing…and two of them were drawn up into the net, leaving them hanging upside down.

Heather came out of the shadows where she'd been hiding. She and Zane sprinted through the trees. Hopefully the third man would be delayed getting the other two out of the net.

They kept moving as evening came on, stopping only to catch their breath or eat a handful of snow while nibbling the jerky Jordan had given them.

The temperature dropped as they made their way up the mountain.

"Don't eat any more snow," Zane instructed at one point. "It will drop your core body temperature." They didn't have time to build a fire and melt some snow. They'd have to go without water.

The climb up the mountain became steeper and more treacherous, slowing their progress. Zane lifted his head. The summit was in sight. He only hoped they were doing the right thing, that Jordan hadn't deceived them and sent them on a wild goose chase. If he had, there would be no way to stop Willis—or for him and Heather to survive.

He prayed he'd made the right choice.

SEVENTEEN

Heather's arm muscles strained as she pulled herself up over a boulder. Their progress slowed to a crawl as they worked their way around rock formations and trudged up steep inclines.

In the dimming evening light, she could see the three men moving along behind them. They were far enough away that they looked like large bugs inching along.

She treaded up a steep incline, choosing where she put her foot carefully. A few rocks rolled down the mountain, banging against each other. Her throat was dry and she longed for a drink of water.

She hoped they hadn't gone on a fool's errand. Zane had a blind spot where his brother was concerned. He so desperately wanted to see Jordan's life turn around.

They came to a wide, sheer cliff face.

Zane put his hands on his hips and took in a breath. "We don't have time to go around this. We'll have to climb it using hand and footholds."

They had no ropes or equipment. The wall was maybe twenty feet high. A fall would probably not kill them, but it could severely injure them. She'd climbed faces like this before, but always with a harness and ropes.

"I'll go first. Follow me," he said.

Heather put her gloves in her pocket so she could grip the rock more easily. Zane worked his way up, moving sideways to find a firm hold. She put her foot into a crevice and reached for the first handhold. The rock was cold to the touch.

Zane was near the top when his foot slipped.

Her breath caught as she held on and watched helplessly. He dangled for a moment before securing another foothold. He pushed himself up and over the top.

Heather worked her way sideways and then up. In the waning light, it was hard to see the holds. She felt around until her fingers found a bump to grip. Zane reached down to pull her up.

His arms wrapped around her, and he drew her close. Her hand rested on his chest as she caught her breath from the exertion. His heart beat beneath her palm. She felt herself relaxing in his embrace, wanting to linger.

He held her a moment longer. "We should probably keep going."

She didn't pull free of his embrace. "Yes, I suppose."

She tilted her head. His finger traced the outline of her jaw and then his lips covered hers. His touch made her feel like she was melting. His strong arms held her as he kissed her more deeply.

He lifted his head but still rested his hand on her cheek. She reached up and pulled a strand of his hair off his forehead, wishing the moment could last forever. She felt light-headed, dizzy even.

Slowly, they separated from each other and came

back to reality. Willis's men were still making their way up the mountain. Willis himself was on his way to blow up a bank. They couldn't stay here forever.

Zane pushed himself to his feet and held out a hand to her. He glanced down the mountain, as well.

"We're not that far from the summit. Let's try to pick up the pace." He touched her face, leaned in and kissed her forehead.

Still a bit wobbly from the first kiss, she nodded. He took off at a jog. She fell in beside him. Her whole body ached from the running they'd done. She longed for water and sleep and warmth. Somehow, though, she found herself realizing that where she really wanted to be was with Zane in whatever conditions. As long as he was by her side, she could endure anything. The top of the mountain came into view. Zane slowed and pulled out the GPS device. He turned a half circle then looked down at the device again.

Down below was the river, and beyond that, the lights of Fort Madison twinkled. The sight renewed her hope. Even after they got across the river, it would be a long hard run through the night to get to town. But still, if Jordan had been telling them the truth about the paragliders, they might make it in time to stop Willis.

She saw no lights or fires along this part of the river that indicated any of Willis's men were waiting for them. That, too, lifted her spirits.

Zane continued to walk around and check their GPS position.

The men were closing in on them from down below. If Jordan had lied, they'd be trapped.

Zane disappeared into the trees. Heather held her

breath and followed, finding Zane on the ground, pushing tree boughs and rocks out of the way.

Heather hurried over and dropped on her knees to help him. All she felt beneath her fingers was dirt.

Zane turned slightly. "Maybe we're just off by a bit."

Tension coiled around Heather's torso. Not just over the fear that Jordan had set them up and that the realization would break Zane's heart, but also at the idea that they were losing precious time while the men who wanted them dead were closing in on them.

Zane picked up a rock and started to tap the ground, listening for a metallic sound. The pounding sounded like a funeral dirge to Heather.

She hit the ground with a rock, too. Though she felt hope slipping away, for Zane's sake, she wouldn't give up either.

And then she heard a metallic echo and joy burst through her. "Here."

Zack shifted toward her, working quickly to clear away the dirt and leaves. The lid creaked when he opened it up, and he pulled out two huge canvas bundles.

"We're going to have to lay them out and attach the harnesses. I'll get started. You go check and see where those men are."

She sprinted out from the shelter of the trees and ran along the ridgeline. The men were jogging up the trail. At the pace they were going, she and Zane had five or maybe ten minutes before they were here. She ran back to where Zane had assembled one of the paragliders and gave her report. He nodded, but kept his focus on the gear in front of him.

"They come together fast," he said. "Help me with the second one."

The paraglider was a nylon wing attached to a harness.

Zane's face was red from exertion. "You ever done anything like this before?"

She nodded. "Once when I was a teenager."

"Go to that high point, get a running start, wait for the wind to lift your parachute. When you come to the edge, take off. The wind will lift you up." He pointed to two strings that came out of either side of the wing. "You steer with these." He picked up one of the paragliders. "Grab yours. I'll help you lay out the parachute."

They hurried out to the high point on the summit where the wind was more intense. Willis's men had just reached the top and were headed in their direction. Her heart raced. Zane saw them, too.

"Let me get you strapped in. Remember, no hesitation once your parachute is up. Take off right away." He kissed her. "I'll fight these guys off and then follow after you if I can. If I don't make it, the way into town will be clear. You need to get down there and warn them."

The thought of losing Zane sent a wave of panic through her but she nodded. This was what had to be done. Once she was strapped into the harness, she grabbed the controls and took in a breath.

"Let me get your leg straps." Zane leaned over and buckled her in. He glanced over his shoulder. The men were within a hundred yards. "Get going."

Zane took several shots at the trio of men. One of them fell to the ground, but the other two kept coming.

She willed herself to look away, shifted focus to the steep incline and took off running, gaining speed. She could see the edge of the cliff. The two men took shots at Zane who scrambled for cover and fired back. In the hurry to get airborne, she'd set her gun down and forgotten it.

Her feet disconnected with the earth. The wind caught the parachute and jerked her skyward. When she glanced backward, she saw that Zane was in a hand-to-hand battle with one of the men.

A current caught her parachute and she drifted even higher. She could see the river down below. Her heart raced at the thought of falling in the freezing water. The weight of the paraglider would drown her. She had to get across.

The wind pushed her down. She steered toward the narrowest part of the river as she lost altitude. She was low enough that she could see the black, cold rapids of the river.

Her feet skimmed the water as she dipped even lower. But she was nearly across. She only needed a little more momentum to reach the other side.

Please God. Help me.

A gust of wind pushed her the remaining distance, landing her on the rocky shore. She unclipped herself from the harness and turned back around, searching the sky for Zane's paraglider.

He had to make it. He just had to.

She tilted her head, gaze darting everywhere. No sign of Zane.

Every minute was precious. How long should she wait before she gave up on Zane and made the final trek into town on her own?

* * *

Zane landed a blow to the last man standing. The other two had been put out of commission with gunshot wounds. He'd managed to get the gun away from the third man. This man, though, fought like a trained fighter, the Bruce Lee of the mountains. Zane could feel himself tiring.

He was grateful that Heather had been able to take off. Even if he died up here, at least she would survive—and there was still a chance they could prevent that bomb from being used.

Bruce slammed a fist into Zane's jaw, and his vision filled with white dots. Zane fought to maintain focus, to not give in to the pain. Bruce came at him again. Zane blocked the shot aimed at his head and punched the other man hard in the stomach so he doubled over. Then Zane landed a blow to his opponent's back, which sent Bruce to his knees. That wouldn't be enough to keep him down long enough for Zane to strap himself into the harness, though. Zane pulled his pistol out and hit the man on the side of the head so he collapsed on his belly.

Zane sprinted up toward where he'd left the paraglider and strapped in. One of the other men—seriously but not fatally wounded from Zane's gunshots—struggled to his feet.

Zane had only precious seconds. When the wind lifted his parachute, he ran down the hill even as the man closed in on him. His feet came to the edge of the cliff. The man reached out to grab him just as his feet separated from the earth. A gunshot broke through the silence of the forest. When he looked up, he saw a small tear in the wing.

Down below, he could see the bright lime and hot pink of Heather's paraglider. She'd made it. He saw no sign of her and wondered if she had chosen to head into town on her own when he'd been delayed. The choice would have been a prudent one.

The wind fluttered the nylon fabric of his parachute. He worked the levers to maintain altitude, hoping to catch another gust of wind. If he dipped down too soon he'd land in the cold water or be forced to land on the wrong side of the river.

He continued to study the landscape below, hoping to catch a glimpse of Heather. Except for those pink gloves, she was dressed head to toe in camo, so it would be easy enough for her to blend into her surroundings.

He shifted his weight to one side, steering to land close to where Heather had. A current lifted him up and then slammed him down even lower. Steering became a challenge as one wing remained lower than the other despite his shifting to balance his weight evenly. He angled his head to examine the parachute. The wind had torn the gash from the bullet, making the tear even larger.

He dropped altitude as he drifted over the river. The mumbling roar of the dark cold waves pressed on his ears. He lifted his feet to avoid getting them wet. The shore was twenty feet away. One side of the wing remained higher than the other as he prepared to land. His feet touched the rocky shore but then he was lifted up again. Momentum forced him to run for some distance before he could stop and click out of his harness.

He turned in a full circle, still hoping to see Heather. He called her name, softly at first and then louder. Half a dozen crows fluttered in the trees and took flight, but Heather didn't answer him. He had to assume that she'd taken off down the trail…or that a squad of Willis's men had been warned by their attackers from the top of the mountain via radio, and Heather had been taken captive or worse.

With no way to know where she was, or if she was even still alive, there was nothing he could do to search for her. And there was still the bank to be protected. The lights of Fort Madison shone down below over several hills and forested areas. He'd have to run all night if he had any hope of getting to town before Willis and his men did. Because of where he'd crossed at the river, he'd be coming into the east side of town instead of the west where the sheriff's office was.

He said a prayer that Heather was all right and on the same path as he was, then he took off jogging.

He'd paced off several miles and rounded a curve when he saw motion up ahead. Heather's porcelain skin shone in the moonlight. He called out to her, and she stopped and turned.

She ran toward him, wrapping her arms around his neck and drawing him close. Her voice filled with exuberance. "I thought you didn't make it." She pulled back to gaze into his eyes.

"'Course I made it." The affection in her voice and the warmth in her eyes made him wish they could stay in the moment forever, but that wasn't possible. "We need to keep moving. We don't have much time."

She nodded. Her arms fell away from his shoulders. She brushed her hand over his cheek, then whirled around and took off running. He fell in behind her. They ran through the night, slowing down from time to time but never stopping.

He was dizzy with fatigue but he pushed himself to keep going.

The sun peeked up over the horizon when they were a few miles from the edge of town.

Zane turned his head as a noise to the east of him caught his attention. ATVs headed in their direction. Heather stuttered in her step.

Of course the pursuers at the top of the mountain had sent word that he and Heather had made it across the river.

Zane scanned the landscape looking for possibilities for escape as the ATVs and armed men bore down on them.

EIGHTEEN

A tightness suctioned around Heather's chest when she saw the lights of the ATVs rapidly approaching. She and Zane were so close to town, so close to being able to stop Willis and his path of destruction.

Zane tugged on her arm and pointed at a cluster of trees that led them off the path.

It was the only choice they had. One of the ATVs switched on a huge searchlight just as they dived into the thick of the forest. With the trees so close together, the men would be forced to search for them on foot.

Zane pulled her deeper into the brush. They were moving away from town instead of toward it, losing ground. How long would they be delayed? Would they be able to get away at all?

The ATVs' engine noise stopped abruptly. That meant the men were at the edge of the forest.

Heather heard a barked command and then a searchlight flooded through the trees. They'd be spotted if they kept running. There were no tall trees to hide in either.

Both of them hurried toward separate hiding places.

Heather slipped in under the thick boughs of a juniper and Zane disappeared behind a bush.

Heather's breath caught as a charge of panic skittered across her nerves.

The bush did not completely hide Zane. She could see his feet.

The voice of the men grew louder and more intense. The searchlight swept the forest floor.

There was no way she could signal Zane without giving herself away. She held her breath.

Zane must have done a final check because he pulled his feet out of view just as the searchers stepped into the clearing.

From her vantage point with her cheek pressed against the ground, Heather caught only glimpses of the men and heard only pieces of their conversation. A pair split off and headed into a different part of the forest. One of those men held the searchlight.

The other two walked in circles close to them, returning twice to where she and Zane were hidden. Her throat went tight with fear.

The men were right next to her, talking in hushed tones. She could see their worn-out combat boots.

She prayed that they wouldn't look too closely under the brush and trees.

"They've got to be hiding. No one runs that fast."

She dared not move or even breathe. The men were so close she could reach out and touch their feet.

"Look around. They've got to be here somewhere." A flashlight clicked on above her.

The light swept over her, but the man did not spot her.

She heard noises from where Zane had hidden.

"There's one of them," the pursuer shouted as he ran away from her. The other followed.

Zane had created a diversion to save her. She hoped he would be able to get away.

Once the men left the area, she slipped out from underneath the juniper and ran toward another bush for cover. She could hear the men shouting at each other, getting farther away from her but closer to Zane.

Please, God, don't let him get caught.

Their voices died away.

She ran from one bush to another, making her way back toward the path they'd been on.

"Heather."

A whisper rose up from off to the side of her. Zane lifted his head above the bush and then ducked back down.

She listened for a moment, not hearing any of the men. She darted toward where Zane was hiding.

He touched her arm lightly. "We have to hurry. I'm sure they will backtrack like I did in a few minutes."

Zane sprinted toward the trail just as the voices rose up behind them.

The men had left their ATVs at the edge of the forest but there were no keys to allow Heather and Zane to take one. They'd have to keep running. Zane hurried down the hill toward town, sticking to the thick brush where the ATVs would have a hard time following.

They ran hard and fast as the sun rose up over the horizon. Behind them, they could hear the ATVs revving up.

It was a struggle to keep moving, but Heather reminded herself that her life depended on it. The lights of the town still looked so far away.

Both of them alerted to noise off to the side, someone coming through the brush at a high rate of speed. They kept running until a braying noise filled the air.

Both of them stopped short as Clarence stepped through the brush. He must have made it across the river after the bridge collapsed. The animal raised and lowered his head, sniggering, then lifted his muzzle and showed his teeth. He looked a little beat up with some scratches on his neck and legs. The mule was thinner but he'd clearly found enough to eat to survive for the past few days.

Heather shook her head as relief spread through her. "I think I love that guy."

Clarence tromped toward them. He still had his bridle, though the saddle must have come loose. But it shouldn't be a problem to ride him bareback, and they'd be able to get into town that much faster.

Zane cupped his hands so Heather could use them as a stirrup to get on Clarence's back. Once she was settled and had the reins in her hands, she angled her foot and held out her hand so Zane could get on behind her.

He pressed in close to her, his breath warming her neck. She spurred Clarence into a trot. As the path evened out, Clarence increased his speed to a gallop.

She could see the edge of town up ahead and hear the ATVs buzzing behind them. They'd be safe once they got into town around people. Clarence trotted past the private residences on the edge of town. Main Street was mostly empty at this early hour.

They dismounted Clarence and headed up the street toward the sheriff's office. The pursuers on the ATVs rolled onto Main Street, as well.

The bank probably wasn't open yet. They didn't

know if the plan was to wait until the bank opened or hit it before. Zane had told her that Willis usually robbed banks when they were closed—but perhaps the delay in getting the bomb ready this time meant that the time frame had changed. There was no way to know for sure.

Fort Madison was a small town of a few hundred people; mostly it was a place for outfitters and fly-fishing guides to meet their clients. No businesses were open at this hour.

Heather felt a tightening in her chest as they turned on the side street where the sheriff's office was.

Zane held a hand out, signaling her to halt. He crouched low and approached the office. All the shades were drawn. He signaled her to follow him around to the other side. Both the sheriff's cars were parked out back.

Zane crouched beneath a window and tried to see under the pulled blind.

Heather glanced around, spotting two parked ATVs.

Zane whispered in her ear. "There's only a sheriff and a deputy for law enforcement for the whole county. It looks like Willis's men might be holding them hostage so they can't respond to the robbery."

Heather's spirits sank. "There's no time to get them free, is there?" It was up to them to stop the madness.

Zane nodded. "We've gotta get down to that bank and fast."

Resolve settled in her belly like a heavy rock as she fought to find the strength and courage to engage in one more battle.

The back door to the sheriff's office burst open. She recognized one of Willis's men, who sprinted toward them as they took off running. Zane led her through alleys and backstreets. She doubted their pursuer would call attention to himself on this quiet morning by shooting at them.

Zane pulled her into the lobby of an abandoned hotel as the man ran past. He pressed against the wall and peered out the dusty window.

"He's coming back," said Zane. He pulled her toward the high check-in counter just as the door creaked open. Footsteps pounded on the wooden floor.

Heather breathed in dust. She pressed her nostrils together to suppress a sneeze. Her heart raced. Zane's back stiffened. The footsteps continued to pound around the lobby, then they heard the squeak of footsteps on the stairs. The noise stopped all together.

Heather held her nose tight. Her eyes watered. The footsteps stomped back toward them. The man came around the counter.

Zane leaped to his feet and charged at the man. The two men punched each other. Zane was backed up to a wall.

Heather searched the area for something to use as a weapon. She picked up a metal pipe and slammed it against the assailant's shoulder. The man turned and lunged at her.

Zane spun him around and hit him hard enough across the jaw that the man fell to the floor.

They ran toward the front of the hotel. Halfway through the revolving door, Zane turned around and swung back into the lobby.

"Men out there, too," he said.

The man on the hotel floor was incapacitated but conscious. Zane hurried past him up the stairs. Heather followed, not sure what Zane had in mind, but he knew this town better than she did.

He led her through the dusty upstairs hallway toward a back room, where he swung open a window. "Climb down." Zane ran over to the door and clicked the lock, probably to keep the man downstairs from getting to them.

Heather stuck her head out the window. There was no fire escape, only a metal trellis. Her heart squeezed tight as she stared at the ground below.

"It's just a matter of minutes before they come around to the back of the hotel," said Zane.

She nodded and slipped out the window. Though it didn't look overly strong, it was only two stories.

The man from downstairs was slamming his body against the locked door, trying to break it down.

She shoved her leg through the window and positioned her foot on the trellis. It creaked as she climbed down it. Zane slipped out of the window before she reached the bottom. He started to climb down. One of the bolts that held the trellis to the brick wall of the hotel broke loose and clattered to the pavement down below.

Heather jumped the remaining feet to the concrete just as the trellis swung away from the wall it was fastened to. More bolts pulled loose and fell out as Zane climbed down.

Heather took in a sharp breath. Men rushed around the side of the hotel. The same men who had been chasing them in the forest. Zane still had fifteen feet to go before he could jump. Another bolt disconnected as the metal trellis swayed.

"Run," Zane shouted at her while he kept descending.

She took off just as Zane jumped the remaining distance to the ground. He dashed after her, with their pursuers hot on their heels.

She had no idea where the bank was. She worked her way back to Main Street, glancing over her shoulder to see if she could spot Zane. No one was there.

She reached Main Street and scanned the dark shops, not seeing the bank. She ran in what she assumed was the direction of the bank, the way they'd been going before.

Zane joined her from a side street. He sprinted in front of her, racing past a garage with dark windows. She saw the bank up ahead, a newer building with a large parking lot.

None of Willis's men stood outside to block their way, so Zane and Heather rushed toward the bank entrance. The bank had large glass doors. Inside a man in a suit ran by in a hurry. She could see a bank teller whose face was stricken with fear and a security guard lying on the floor.

Zane reached out for the door handle. It was locked.

Heather couldn't see any of Willis's men inside. Yet it was clear they'd been there and had disabled the security guard and locked the building.

Zane pounded on the glass, trying to get the bank teller's attention. She continued to stare at the fallen bank guard.

He took a step back. "Maybe there's an employees-only entrance that's open."

Her heartbeat thudded in her ears. "Willis's men must be in there even if we can't see them."

Everything seemed to be moving in slow motion. Even Zane's response felt delayed. "I know that."

The men who had been chasing them entered the parking lot but remained at the edge of the pavement.

A stillness seemed to fall on them like a heavy blanket. Heather heard a percussive boom followed by an echo. Glass shattered around her as she felt herself being lifted up and thrown back by a hot, forceful wind.

NINETEEN

Zane felt his body turning in space. The heat and light of the explosion surrounded him. He couldn't tell up from down until his back hit the hard pavement of the parking lot. He slid for several feet. He registered pain in his back. Glass showered down on him and he lifted his arm over his face to shield himself. He couldn't hear anything, though he saw men running inside the bank and knew that alarms must be going off. But no one would answer the alarms. The sheriff was being held captive. There was no other law in Fort Madison. Even the volunteer fire department would be slow in arriving. He had to find a way to keep Willis from getting away with this.

The thermite bomb wouldn't have caused such an explosion. Willis must have had an additional bomb designed to do damage and maybe even hurt people. He glanced across the street. With the bomb primed to do that much damage, the bomber wouldn't have wanted to set it off manually, so it must have been remotely detonated. Was the triggerman hovering close by?

Zane scanned the area for anyone looking suspicious, but instead spotted Heather laying on her back and not moving. He pushed himself to his feet, stared at his bloody palms then he ran toward her prone body. He turned her over. She opened her eyes and said something to him, but he couldn't hear it.

He shook his head, still trying to orient himself. The men who had been in the parking lot ran into the bank through the broken glass of the doors. He saw then that the steel vault had been blown completely open as the men drilled the safety deposit boxes and emptied the contents. They seemed to be selective in the boxes they chose, consulting the man in the suit who was being held at gunpoint.

He didn't see Willis anywhere. He must be waiting outside of town for the loot to be brought to him.

He helped Heather to her feet. Glass cascaded off her clothes and hair. She had a gash across her forehead. He knew that she continued to shout at him from the way her mouth moved, but it felt like he had cotton balls in his ears.

Two of the men came out of the bank, each holding a small duffel. One of the men was Jordan. Jordan jumped in a Jeep and took off out of the parking lot, not even noticing Zane and Heather.

Zane could not process what he was seeing. What was Jordan doing?

Heather continued to shout at him and point at a place outside of town toward the foothills. Her expression was frantic. She placed her face very close to his and mouthed the words again as she gripped his upper arm.

Finally, his ears cleared out. Her voice seemed to echo and sound far away at the same time.

"I saw a helicopter land over there. It's the direction Jordan is driving."

It stung to hear Jordan's name. Why had Jordan helped them just to participate in the robbery in the end? Had Jordan simply tried to save his brother while his loyalty remained with Willis? Zane collected his thoughts and pushed down the confusion that threatened to overtake him. "That must be Willis's escape plan to get out of here with the loot."

"We need to get over there and stop them."

The robbers had already disappeared, probably headed back up to the high country or some new hiding place before they could get caught. Maybe Willis had set up some sort of rendezvous point.

Zane glanced around. They needed a car, and fast. There were several parked in the corner of the lot that remained undamaged by the blast. Zane ran into the bank, his boots treading over broken glass.

The bank teller was on the phone touching her hands to her face and talking rapidly. The man in the suit who must be the bank manager was bent over the security guard.

Zane stepped over the debris. The room still hadn't cleared of the dust. "Are those your cars out there? I need keys. I can catch the guy who did this."

The bank manager pulled keys from his pocket and tossed them to Zane. "It's the silver Honda." He stared down at the prone security guard, his voice filled with concern. "The ambulance has to drive all the way from Badger. It will take an hour." He shook his head. "Why didn't Sheriff Smith come?"

Zane didn't have time to answer the man's questions. "Can I have his gun?"

Hopefully the volunteer fire department would get here faster to help.

The bank manager was so dazed he wasn't even questioning who Zane was. He pulled the gun from the unconscious security guard's holster and slid it across the floor. Zane picked up the gun.

Zane stepped over the broken glass and out into the early-morning sun. Heather waited for him. He handed her the gun. "I saw you didn't have yours." He pointed toward the car. "Over there."

They both ran to the car. He unlocked it, and she got into the passenger side. He knew the road that would take them up to where the helicopter had landed. He shifted into Reverse and hit the accelerator, burning rubber as he left the parking lot and zoomed out onto the two lane road.

Heather gripped the armrest. Zane pushed the car to go faster up the country road. Anxiety encroached on his thoughts. He didn't want to have a showdown with his brother. But he might not have a choice.

They rounded a curve. He could see the bright red of the helicopter in the brush up ahead. He slowed the car and pulled off to the side. "Best if we approach on foot. You stay back."

"You might need my help," she said.

They didn't have time to argue. He clicked open the door. "Use your best judgment." They'd been through enough that he knew she'd be smart about what she did. She knew when to take a risk and when to refrain. And there was no one he trusted more at his back.

Zane bent over and hurried along the road. Heather followed but at a distance. The helicopter came into view again. He dived to the ground and watched. Only one man paced beside the chopper, someone he didn't recognize. He must be the pilot.

The Jeep was parked to one side, but Jordan and Willis were nowhere in sight. What was going on here?

Zane craned his neck and noticed that Heather was no longer behind him. She must have slipped into the brush to have a different vantage point. Zane moved in a little closer. Now was his chance to take the pilot out while Jordan and Willis weren't around.

As soon as the pilot turned his back, Zane pulled the gun and sprinted. He hit the pilot on the side of the head. Zane caught him and laid him on the ground. He saw Heather now on the other side of the chopper, hiding in the grass. The two bags from the bank were already loaded on the chopper.

He scanned the foothills. Jordan and Willis had left to go get something—maybe more loot, such as the profits from the marijuana sales or some other theft they'd committed.

Heather continued to hide in the brush. Zane crouched by the chopper and scanned the hills all around him.

Cold metal touched the back of his head.

Willis's voice cut him to the core. "I don't think you're going anywhere today."

Heather watched in horror as Willis put a gun to Zane's head. Jordan stood behind Willis, holding a metal box that was covered in dirt.

"The pilot is out," said Jordan.

"I see that. Revive him." Willis kept his gun on Zane's head as he reached down, pulled Zane's gun out of his waistband and tossed it aside.

Heather's heart pounded against her rib cage as she gripped the gun. She wasn't that good a shot. If she missed, Willis would shoot Zane right away. She needed to be closer.

Jordan disappeared inside the chopper and then poked his head out and walked over to the pilot. What was Jordan up to? Was he really just going to let Willis shoot Zane after he'd helped get them safe across the river? She could only guess that a split loyalty had driven Jordan's choices. The younger brother had probably never imagined it coming down to this.

She had to act quickly. She moved in closer trying to line up a better shot.

Jordan worked to revive the helicopter pilot by slapping his cheeks.

"March away from the chopper over to those trees," Willis commanded Zane. "All of this could have been yours if you had stuck with me. Now your brother gets the lion's share."

Jordan stopped and looked up, but then returned to reviving the pilot.

Heather scrambled out and lifted the gun. She stood on her feet, aimed the sights toward Willis and pulled the trigger.

Willis stopped short and spun around. She didn't know if she'd hit him or not. He raised his handgun at Heather. Jordan jumped up, placing himself between Heather and Willis. Willis either didn't notice or didn't care as he pulled the trigger. Jordan crumpled to the ground.

Heather screamed.

She dived down to help Jordan as another shot was fired. Jordan opened his eyes and smiled at her. She reached up to his neck where she still felt a pulse, but blood seeped out of his side onto the ground.

When she looked up, Zane had taken advantage of Willis's momentary distraction to jump him from behind. Willis's gun was in the brush and the two men wrestled in hand-to-hand combat.

Zane was going to have to deal with Willis without her help. She kept her focus on Jordan, who needed medical attention fast. She said his name several times before he focused on her.

"You've been hit," she said.

Jordan gripped her arm as he struggled to get the words out. "I was going to stop him. I was the only one who could. Just had to wait for the right moment. So sorry it had to go this far. Never had the chance. Willis must have sensed something."

So that had been the plan.

"I'm going to get you to a hospital." She laid him down gently on the ground.

"Sorry for what I did to you." Jordan's voice was weak as he turned his head to one side and closed his eyes.

Heather ran over to the parked Jeep. The keys were still in the ignition. She fired up the engine and drove it to where Jordan lay prone and bleeding out.

The helicopter pilot had just started to stir. She remembered what the bank manager had said about an ambulance having to come from far away. Jordan didn't have that kind of time.

She ran over to the pilot, hoping and praying that he had no loyalty to Willis, that he was just hired help. He was blinking rapidly and rubbing the side of his head, but he didn't seem hostile, just looked up at her with a puzzled expression when she approached.

"You have to take me and this man to the hospital in Badger."

"That's not what I was hired to do."

She gripped his collar and drew him close to her face. "Your orders have changed. Help me lift this man on that chopper." She spoke in a tone that meant business, hoping that would keep the pilot from arguing.

The pilot threw up his hands. "I don't care as long as I get paid."

Jordan moaned as they lifted him into the backseat. Heather crawled in beside him to keep pressure on his wound.

The blades of the chopper sliced through the air as the pilot fired up the engine. She couldn't see Zane or Willis anywhere. Their hand-to-hand battle must have taken them into the trees.

The helicopter lifted off. She wrapped her arms around Jordan and whispered in his ear, "It's going to be all right."

"Zane?"

"He's going to be okay, too. You did good."

As she searched the ground down below and saw nothing, she prayed she was telling the truth on both counts.

TWENTY

Zane could feel years of pent-up rage smoldering and growing hotter as he lifted his hand to hit Willis across the jaw. Willis blocked his punch. Willis had extensive martial arts training, and though he was older than Zane, his skill level was much higher. Not to mention Zane was exhausted after hard days of being chased through the mountains with limited supplies and little rest.

Zane spent way more time dodging blows than he did delivering them as Willis backed him into the high brush.

He could hear the helicopter taking off. He'd caught a glimpse of Heather and the pilot loading Jordan into the backseat. Jordan had stepped between Heather and Willis's bullet. Why he'd played along with Willis's schemes to this point was anyone's guess, but it was clear now where his loyalty lay. He prayed his brother would be all right.

For Jordan and for all the young men who'd been led astray, he wanted Willis to go to jail. Willis swung his leg for a high kick. Zane ducked out of the way as rage boiled over inside him. He lifted his hand to land a blow, but Willis reached up to block it. He switched to the other arm and then double punched Willis. The sudden move caused Willis to take a few steps back.

Zane charged toward him and knocked him to the ground. They rolled until Willis was on top. Willis hit Zane twice across the jaw, first with one fist and then with the other. The blows left Zane stunned and unable to focus. Willis got to his feet and dashed off through the brush.

Zane shook off the dizziness and bolted to his feet. When he came out from the brush, Willis was perched in the Jeep, turning the key in the ignition. The Jeep was backed up and then Willis shifted, lurching forward and then gaining speed on the dirt road to rumble past Zane.

Zane ran to catch up with it, pushing his tired legs to go faster. He jumped in the back of the Jeep. Willis shot over his shoulder without looking. He must have had a gun in the car. The bullet hit the metal sides of the car. The car swerved and Zane was nearly thrown out. He plunged to his knees and inched toward the driver's seat.

Willis placed the pistol on his shoulder again while he kept his eyes on the road. Zane flattened himself as another shot reverberated through the air.

Willis pulled out onto the main road and increased his speed. Zane struggled to get upright as the wind rushed around him. Willis jerked the wheel back and forth in an attempt to throw Zane out.

Zane held on and crawled toward Willis, who held the gun in one hand and drove with the other. That left him without any hand free to protect himself from attack. Zane wrapped his arm around Willis's neck, so

Willis's chin was in the crook of Zane's elbow. Zane squeezed.

Willis slowed down but lifted the gun.

Zane released Willis from the neck lock and lunged for the gun. His hand wrapped around it as the car veered into the other lane and down a bank. The Jeep rolled, landing upside down. Zane was thrown free and impacted with the hard ground as he stared up at the bed of the Jeep. Metal creaked all around him.

Zane flipped over to his stomach and crawled out from underneath the Jeep, grateful that the roll bars had kept him from being crushed. Willis was not in the driver's seat. Zane pushed himself into a sitting position and looked around. Willis was running away up the ditch, favoring one foot. He worked his way up the bank and stuck his thumb out for a ride.

This man was not going to get away, not on Zane's watch. Zane pushed himself to his feet, groaning from the bruising his legs and arms had taken in the crash. All the same, he ran hard to catch up with Willis as a car drew nearer on the road and started to slow down.

Willis ran a little ways down the road. The car came to a stop. Willis reached for the passenger-side door. Zane pumped his legs even harder. Willis got into the car. It rolled into motion just as Zane grabbed the passenger-side door handle and yanked it open.

The driver shouted in protest.

"Go, this man is a lunatic," Willis said as he reached to click his seat belt in place.

Zane grabbed Willis and pulled him out of the car as the surprised driver hit the brakes. Willis rolled down the bank and Zane lunged after him as the images of his brother and the other young men flashed before his eyes. He landed enough blows to Willis's face and stomach to debilitate him.

Zane was out of breath as he stood over Willis, who drew his legs up toward his stomach and struggled for air.

"Is there something I can do?" the driver of the car, a fortysomething man, shouted from the road.

"This is the man who needs to be arrested...not me," Zane called back. "He just robbed the bank and is trying to make a getaway."

The light of understanding came into the man's eyes and he nodded.

"Do you have a cell phone? Please call the sheriff. This man needs to be taken into custody." He doubted the sheriff was still being held hostage.

"Yes, I do." The driver returned to his car.

Zane stood over Willis, ready to subdue him if he decided to fight back or run. He heard sirens in the distance.

Willis caught his breath but remained on the ground with his legs drawn up to his stomach. "Maybe you won this round. But I wasn't at the bank. Your brother was. He'll be the one going to jail...if he makes it."

Zane felt as though a sword had been stabbed through his gut. What would happen to Jordan was still uncertain. He only hoped that Heather had been able to get him medical help fast enough.

Heather sat on the hard plastic chairs of the hospital waiting room. Jordan had been wheeled in for emergency surgery as soon as the chopper had landed. That was over an hour ago. She'd talked to the police in Badger but they didn't know where Zane was.

Her chest felt like it was in a vise being squeezed tighter and tighter. Jordan had risked his life to save hers. She wasn't sure what she would do if he didn't make it. It would tear Zane to pieces, too. Her heart squeezed even tighter. If Zane had made it himself. What if Willis hurt or killed Zane and then got away? She could not bear the idea of the loss and the injustice of it all.

A nurse in scrubs came out into the waiting room. "You're the woman who came in with Jordan Scofield."

Heather jumped to her feet. "Yes."

"His next of kin is not here?"

Heather shook her head. "Um… I'm hoping he'll be here soon."

"I guess I can tell you. Jordan came through the surgery. We were able to stop the bleeding and remove the bullet. He should be waking up shortly."

Heather nodded, not sure what to say.

"As soon as his next of kin gets here, please let us know." The nurse turned on her heels and disappeared around a corner.

Heather sank back down into her seat, feeling numb. Though the news about Jordan had lifted her spirits, anxiety plagued her thoughts. What would she do if Zane didn't make it? She'd thought she'd be on a plane back to California by now, leaving Montana behind her, but that wasn't an option anymore. So much had changed.

Even with all the danger, there was something special about the high country of Montana and something even more special about Zane. She wasn't that crazy about getting on the plane anymore.

She stared up at the television that was on in the

waiting room. A local news story flashed on the screen. She saw a Jeep overturned in a road—Willis's Jeep.

Her heart racing she hurried over to the receptionist. "How do you turn the sound up on that TV?"

The receptionist lifted the remote and pointed it. The sound of the local newscaster filled the room. There were shots of the sheriff's car and Willis being led away in handcuffs, but none of Zane. The female newscaster signed out. "Reporting for KBLK in Fort Madison, this is Elizabeth Tan Creti."

Her spirits sank. What had happened to Zane?

She felt a hand on her shoulder.

"I always was a little bit camera shy."

The sound of Zane's voice filled her with exhilaration. She fell against his chest and he wrapped his arms around her. She took in a breath and relaxed for the first time since she'd gotten on the chopper. Zane had made it.

"Jordan?"

She pulled back and looked up into his eyes glowing with affection. "He's just waking up from the surgery. We can go see him in a bit."

Zane nodded. She reached up and lightly touched the scratch on his face.

"Took quite a bit to get Willis under control."

"But you did it."

He brushed a strand of hair out of her eyes. "We did it."

The word *we* echoed through her brain. They made a pretty good team. She felt pulled in two directions. Her whole life was in California.

The nurse came around the corner. "Jordan is awake. You can see him." She glanced at Zane. "You must be the next of kin. Brother, right? I see the resemblance. He's in room 212."

Zane nodded. He grabbed Heather's hand. "I want you to come with me."

The walk down the long hospital corridor seemed to take forever as they made their way to Jordan's room. What kind of future lay ahead for Jordan? Clearly his loyalty was no longer with Willis, but he had been under the other man's control for so long. Getting free of that kind of brainwashing would take time and hard work.

The two of them stood outside room 212. Heather took in a breath and prayed for a healed relationship between the brothers and clarity on why she was so conflicted about going back to California.

TWENTY-ONE

Heather and Zane stood on the summit where her father had wanted his ashes spread. The landscape took Heather's breath away. From this vantage point, she had almost a 360-degree view of the area. She could see Fort Madison off in the distance and the river winding its way through the valley.

"I see why my father loved this spot," she said.

Zane had kept his word and helped her fulfill her father's last wish, a week later than planned.

Zane stepped closer to her. "He told me he came up here to pray. He said you could see all of God's creation for miles."

Zane had made a sacrifice to take her up here so quickly. Jordan was still in the hospital. He was going to be okay physically. While he would be held accountable for the crimes he had committed over the past several years, the sheriff seemed to think Jordan would receive a light sentence in exchange for testifying against Willis.

Heather walked over to Clarence and pulled the thin wooden box out of his saddlebag. "I suppose I should do what I came to Montana to do in the first place."

The words weighed heavy in the air. So much had happened since the day they'd taken off for the high country. All the assumptions she had made about Zane had been wrong. Everything she thought she knew about her father had been turned upside down.

Zane came and stood beside her. "Did you make your plane reservations for going home?"

"I thought I'd wait. I still have to meet with Dennis Havre."

His tone darkened to bit. "Right, to sell Big Sky Outfitters."

That had been her plan all along—to sell and then get back on an airplane, never to see Montana again. "Yes." She felt a tugging at her heart. What had seemed like the right thing to do a week and a half ago now turned her stomach in knots.

Zane ran his fingers through his hair and shifted his weight from side to side. "I don't have the money to buy Big Sky Outfitters, but maybe we could work out some kind of payment plan? I care more about protecting the legacy of your father's reputation than Dennis does. That has to mean something."

She saw the pain in Zane's eyes. "Of course it does." She had come to respect what he did for a living and to love the high country. She stared down at the box then clicked it open. Her breath caught. There were no ashes inside.

Zane stepped toward her.

Inside the box was a stack of letters addressed to her. She recognized her mother's handwriting where she had written "return to sender."

Tears warmed the corners of her eyes. "He *did* try to have contact with me."

"Whatever your mother's reasons for not wanting you to know him, I want you to understand that he was a changed man by the time he came into my life."

"I know that now because of who you are. Without my father's influence you would have been like one of those young men who chose to believe Willis's lies."

He kissed her forehead. "I'm going to miss you, Heather. Please consider my offer to let me buy Big Sky Outfitters over time."

She gazed at the man in front of her as the mountain breeze whirled around her and the expanse of God's creation was laid out before her. She knew then that she loved him, and loved this place. "I have a better idea. What if we ran it together? Do you think you could teach me how to be a guide?"

He let out a breath as the corners of his mouth turned up and light came into his eyes. "You've already proved to me you have the mettle to survive under the most traumatic of circumstances. I'd be proud to take you on. But I'd like to be more than just business partners."

She tilted her head.

"I'd like you to be my wife." His fingers touched her temple and trailed across her cheeks. The face looking at her was full of love.

Her own heart burst with joy and she knew what her answer was. "Yes, Zane Scofield. I will marry you."

He wrapped an arm around her waist and drew her close. They stared out at the natural beauty that spread out before them. Trees, rivers and mountains, everything her father had loved.

"Do you suppose my father wanted you to guide me to this spot because he thought we might hit it off?"

"I wouldn't put it past him." Zane kissed the top of her head. "He was smart that way."

She stared down at the letters, knowing that she would get to know the man who had brought she and Zane together even better by reading what he had written her.

Heather tilted her head and looked into the eyes of the man she wanted to spend the rest of her life with. He leaned in and kissed her.

* * * * *

If you loved this story,
don't miss these other exciting books from
Sharon Dunn:

MONTANA STANDOFF
WILDERNESS TARGET
COLD CASE JUSTICE
MISTAKEN TARGET
FATAL VENDETTA

Find more great reads at www.LoveInspired.com.

Dear Reader,

I hope you enjoyed going on the wild ride with Zane and Heather as they faced danger together and found a way to each other's hearts. *Big Sky Showdown* is more than a love story filled with suspense, though. It is the tale of two fathers and the two men whose lives were changed by their influence. Willis controls Jordan through fear and punishment and the promise of promotion. Stephan transformed Zane's life by spending time with him and loving him. While it is possible to gain obedience from someone through shaming and fear, only love and grace can change the human heart. Heather's father was a human being who, before he became a Christian, hurt the people he loved because of his destructive choices. Heather had a great deal of pain because of her father's legacy and her mother's bitterness. Even people who love us often hurt us. When I am faced with that reality, I am so grateful that we have a Father who loves us unconditionally, is faithful and keeps His promises.

Sharon Dunn

REQUEST YOUR FREE BOOKS!

2 FREE RIVETING INSPIRATIONAL NOVELS
PLUS 2 FREE MYSTERY GIFTS

Love Inspired®
SUSPENSE
RIVETING INSPIRATIONAL ROMANCE

YES! Please send me 2 FREE Love Inspired® Suspense novels and my 2 FREE mystery gifts (gifts are worth about $10). After receiving them, if I don't wish to receive any more books, I can return the shipping statement marked "cancel." If I don't cancel, I will receive 4 brand-new novels every month and be billed just $4.99 per book in the U.S. or $5.49 per book in Canada. That's a savings of at least 17% off the cover price. It's quite a bargain! Shipping and handling is just 50¢ per book in the U.S. and 75¢ per book in Canada.* I understand that accepting the 2 free books and gifts places me under no obligation to buy anything. I can always return a shipment and cancel at any time. Even if I never buy another book, the two free books and gifts are mine to keep forever.

123/323 IDN GH5Z

Name _____ (PLEASE PRINT)

Address _____ Apt. #

City _____ State/Prov. _____ Zip/Postal Code

Signature (if under 18, a parent or guardian must sign)

Mail to the **Reader Service:**
IN U.S.A.: P.O. Box 1867, Buffalo, NY 14240-1867
IN CANADA: P.O. Box 609, Fort Erie, Ontario L2A 5X3

**Are you a current subscriber to Love Inspired® Suspense books
and want to receive the larger-print edition?
Call 1-800-873-8635 or visit www.ReaderService.com.**

* Terms and prices subject to change without notice. Prices do not include applicable taxes. Sales tax applicable in N.Y. Canadian residents will be charged applicable taxes. Offer not valid in Quebec. This offer is limited to one order per household. Not valid for current subscribers to Love Inspired Suspense books. All orders subject to credit approval. Credit or debit balances in a customer's account(s) may be offset by any other outstanding balance owed by or to the customer. Please allow 4 to 6 weeks for delivery. Offer available while quantities last.

Your Privacy—The Reader Service is committed to protecting your privacy. Our Privacy Policy is available online at www.ReaderService.com or upon request from the Reader Service.
We make a portion of our mailing list available to reputable third parties that offer products we believe may interest you. If you prefer that we not exchange your name with third parties, or if you wish to clarify or modify your communication preferences, please visit us at www.ReaderService.com/consumerchoice or write to us at Reader Service Preference Service, P.O. Box 9062, Buffalo, NY 14240-9062. Include your complete name and address.

LIS15

"I looked up the license plate of the black sedan from the restaurant," Miles said, his expression grim. "The sedan is registered to Sci-Tech."

"They sent gunmen after us?" Paige asked in a strained whisper.

"Yeah, that's what it looks like."

"They're after me because of my ex-husband, aren't they?"

"I think so, yes." Miles reached over and cradled her icy hands in his. "I'm sorry."

Paige gripped his hands tightly. "You have to find Travis before it's too late."

He didn't want to point out that it might already be too late. Whatever Abby had seen on the tablet had frightened her to the point she wouldn't speak. Had Travis told her to keep quiet? Or had she seen something horrible? He found himself hoping for the first option, but feared the latter.

"I'm not sure where to look for Travis," he admitted. "There's no way to know where he'd go to hide if he thought he was in danger."

"Did you give the police the list of names I gave you?" Paige asked. "I know they're only a few names, but…"

"I've been searching on their names, but I haven't found anything yet. At least we have another link to Sci-Tech. No wonder they were stonewalling me."

"I might be able to get inside the building," Paige offered.

"No." His knee-jerk reaction surprised him, and he tried to backpedal. "I mean, if they're the ones behind this, then it's not safe for you to go there. Besides, how would you get in?"

She lifted her uncertain gaze to his. "I know a couple of the security guards pretty well. If I waited until after-hours, when there's only one security guard manning the desk, I might be able to convince them to let me in."

"I know you want to help, but it's not worth the risk." He couldn't stand the idea of Paige walking into the equivalent of the lion's den. "You don't know for sure which security guard would be on duty. And besides, if anything happened—Abby would be lost without you."

She blinked, and he thought he saw the glint of tears. "Logically, I know you're right, but it's hard to sit back and do nothing, not even trying."

"I'll find a way to do something while keeping you and Abby safe." He couldn't stand the thought of her worrying about things she couldn't change. He'd protect her, no matter what.

Don't miss
THE ONLY WITNESS
by Laura Scott, available February 2017 wherever
Love Inspired® Suspense books and ebooks are sold.

www.LoveInspired.com

LISEXP0117